DEVLIN

WERE ZOO BOOK FIVE

R. E. BUTLER

Devlin (Were Zoo Book Five)

By R. E. Butler

Copyright 2017 R. E. Butler

DEVLIN (WERE ZOO BOOK FIVE)
BY R. E. BUTLER

This book is licensed for your personal enjoyment only. This book may not be re-sold or given away to other people. If you would like to share this book with another person, please purchase an additional copy for each recipient. If you're reading this book and did not purchase it, or it was not purchased for your use only, then please purchase your own copy. Thank you for respecting the hard work of the author.

Cover by CT Cover Designs

This ebook is a work of fiction. Names, characters, places, and incidents are the product of the author's imagination and not to be construed as real. Any resemblance to actual persons, living or dead, events or locations is coincidental.
Disclaimer: The material in this book is for mature audiences only and contains graphic sexual content and is intended for those older than the age of 18 only.

~

Edited by Tracy Vincent

∽

*Thanks to Shelley for beta-reading and making me think.
Much love to Joyce, the bestest bestie on the planet, who remembers
everything I don't, and calls me on it with love and a little sarcasm.
For BB and BL - I love you both.*

Devlin (Were Zoo Book Five)
By R. E. Butler

Lion shifter, Jenni Brisban, is beginning to think that the VIP tours hosted by the Amazing Adventures Safari Park aren't going to help her find her soulmate. Hardly any human males come on the tour, and she spends her weekends in her shift, feeling like her life is passing before her eyes. When she's offered a job in the new sweets shop at the park, she decides that standing behind the counter, talking to customers, and sneaking candy is just what she needs to get her mind off her singleness.

Human, Devlin Potter, is poised to get a promotion at work that will change his life dramatically. Finally, all his hard work will be worth it. The job he wants is just within reach, and his five-year plan is right on track. But when he sees a beautiful blonde woman at his cousin's sweets shop, everything he ever thought he wanted disappears in a hot flash. Now, he only wants Jenni.

Nothing is hotter to Devlin than being with Jenni, but he can tell she's holding something back. When he comes to the zoo to see her, but finds himself at the lion paddock, staring into a lioness's eyes that are the same pretty blue as Jenni's, he knows exactly what her secret is, even though it seems impossible. Devlin has a choice to make: give up everything to live with Jenni at the zoo, or walk away forever. She can't live in his world, but can he live in hers?

CHAPTER ONE

Jenni Brisban finished braiding her long hair and secured the end with an elastic band. She tucked her work shirt into her khaki shorts and slipped her feet into tennis shoes, then headed to the kitchen to fill her travel mug with coffee. She wasn't normally a morning person, but since she started working at the new sweets shop in the Amazing Adventures Safari Park, she'd begun to get used to the early mornings.

The park was owned and operated by shifters who kept their animal natures carefully hidden from humans. Jenni was one of eight lions in the pride that called the park home. The pride was her only family, taking over for the mother who'd chosen to leave them and the then twelve-year-old Jenni to become the alpha female of another pride. Like real lions, the alpha didn't want the child of another male around, leaving Jenni unwelcome there. She'd been heartbroken by her mother's decision, but the pride rallied around her and became her surrogate family: the alpha, Caesar, was the father she'd never known, and the others were the brothers who drove her crazy.

After fixing her coffee the way she liked it, with vanilla creamer and an extra spoonful of sugar, she walked out of her home and headed to work. Her home was underground, in the pride's private living area. The floor was a cushiony material the color of dried grass, the walls were painted to mimic the savannah, and the ceiling was wired with lights to give the illusion of sunlight. Each group that called Amazing Adventures home had a private area. The groups were linked through a central marketplace underground. Among the other shifter groups in the zoo were bears, wolves, elephants, and gorillas.

"Hey, Jenni," Xavier called as she left her home.

The lions worked security for the park and up until recently, Jenni had, too. But she'd grown tired of the security office, watching the monitors and patrolling the park, and had been excited to take a job making candy.

"Morning," she said.

He waited for her at the door that led out of the private area to the hallway. Each shifter group had two ways to get topside—a general staircase that led to a hidden entrance in the employee cafeteria, or a private set of stairs that would lead up to a storage shed in each group's paddock. They spent time in their shifts nearly every day, so that visitors to the park could enjoy the safari tour.

"What are you making in the shop today?" he asked, holding the door open for her.

"Taffy. It seems to be my specialty."

He made a face. "Not banana taffy."

She laughed. Lexy, who was human and mated to Win, one of the gorilla shifters, made a lot of banana flavored treats, including taffy. The sweets shop had been closed for years, after the mated couple who had run it opted to retire. Lexy opened the shop, and invited Jenni to help make candy, along with Lexy's best friend, Trina.

The shop was having a private event that night for the zoo, and Lexy and Trina's families were coming. The shop would officially open to the public on Friday morning.

"No more banana taffy, we've got about fifty pounds of it. Today I'm making watermelon and lemon."

"Cool," Xavier said.

They climbed up the stairs to the employee cafeteria. The bear shifters handled the food in the zoo, from the marketplace, where their people could get meals to the cafeteria for when they were on duty. She stopped next to Xavier at the long counter, where heat lamps kept freshly-made breakfast sandwiches warm, and selected a bacon and egg bagel.

"What's going on in security?" she asked as she opened the wrapper and took a bite.

Xavier grabbed two sandwiches and walked with her out of the building. "Nothing new. We added new security cameras around the perimeter of the park, and there are more monitors in the security office. Do you miss us?"

She snorted. "Don't take it personally, but no."

He shot her a grin. "It must be nice to be around girls instead of just guys."

"That's an understatement."

Jenni was the only lioness in the pride. Jupiter, Caesar's oldest son, was mated to a human female named Celeste, but she and Jenni were still getting to know each other.

"See ya later," Xavier said.

Jenni waved goodbye, leaving Xavier at the security office. She headed down a path to the sweets shop called Lexy's Sweet Treasures. It was a few minutes until six and Jenni could see that the lights were already on in the shop. She hurried her steps, finishing her sandwich before she reached the door. The bell over the door tinkled as she pushed it open.

"Morning," she called out.

"I'm back here," Lexy said. "Trina is on her way."

Jenni walked through the swinging door that led to the commercial kitchen and found Lexy at one of the huge stand mixers, adding chunks of butter to the bowl.

"What are you making?" Jenni asked as she dropped her wrapper in the trash and went to wash her hands.

"Sugar cookies. I have these cute cookie cutters that look like all the animals here. I'll cook them with sticks in them so they'll be like a cookie lollipop."

"Sounds adorable." Jenni put her yellow apron on and tied it at her back.

"How was your night?"

"Fine."

She turned on the taffy machine and took one of the tablets that they kept on hand for recipes, locating the recipe for lemon taffy. As she gathered the ingredients, Lexy said, "Just fine?"

"Yeah. I'm just... can I be honest with you?"

"Oh gosh, you're not going to quit already, are you? I love having you here!" Lexy looked positively panicked.

"No, of course not! I'm just feeling lonely."

"Oh," Lexy said. "Good. Well, I don't mean *good*, I mean, I'm glad you're not quitting. The VIP tours aren't producing mates like the council thought they would, huh?"

"Unfortunately, not."

Because shifters were unknown to humans, they couldn't just meet someone and tell them everything about their people. The carefully guarded secret was important to the safety of shifters everywhere. Their kind believed in soulmates, that there was one person in the world for every shifter, and meeting that person was like love at first sight. One glimpse of their mate, and their beast was ready to settle down.

Fewer and fewer of their people were finding their soulmates, and the council—made up of the alphas of each group—had decided to send out coupons to eligible males and females in the tri-state area for their VIP tours. They were hopeful that their people would find their mates on the tours, but so far, only two males had found theirs from the tour—Zane and Jupiter. Win and Justus had also found mates, only through chance meetings, one via flat tire and one from the sweets shop.

"There are four new mates now. I think it's a good sign," Lexy said.

Jenni hoped so, but she wasn't feeling super positive at the moment. Hardly any males came on the VIP tour, so Friday, Saturday, and Sunday, she would be in her shift and watching Jeep after Jeep of females come by.

"I hope so."

"What are we hoping for?" Trina asked as she walked into the kitchen.

"For Jenni to find her soulmate soon," Lexy answered.

"Aw. I'm sure it'll happen. What guy wouldn't want to be with a beautiful lioness like you?"

Jenni's cheeks heated at the compliment and she smiled. "I'll just keep my fingers crossed."

"And toes," Trina said, "for good luck."

"Meanwhile," Lexy said, "let's get on with the morning. The party will be here before we know it."

Jenni turned her attention to the recipe for lemon taffy and pushed the thoughts of finding her soulmate to the far corner of her mind. Part of her knew that she'd find him at the right time and that she couldn't hurry fate. But most of her, the pacing anxious lioness, wanted to find him right now so they could get started with the next chapter of their lives.

Together.

CHAPTER TWO

Devlin Potter let his mind wander as he waited for the coffee to finish brewing. He had a million things on his mind, the most important one being whether he was going to be offered the promotion in the accounting firm. He'd just graduated from college with his masters in accounting. Numbers had always fascinated him, and although a lot of people thought math was boring, he enjoyed it. He'd been with Frindhim Associates since he received his associates degree several years earlier, slowly moving up the ranks until he'd reached Assistant Controller.

But the job he wanted was for the newly vacated position of Controller. Just beyond that was Assistant Vice President of Finance and then Vice President. He had a five-year career plan and currently he was right on track.

After fixing his coffee, he returned to his cubicle and opened the financials to begin work. As the day slipped by, he wondered if he'd been passed up for the promotion.

His desk phone rang and he answered.

"Hey Devlin, can you come in my office, please?" Harry

Frindhim, the president of the company said when Devlin answered.

"Sure thing, Mr. Frindhim."

His heart jumped into his throat as excitement rippled through him. Heading to the corner office, he knocked on the door and opened it. The Vice President and Assistant Vice President were sitting across the desk from Mr. Frindhim. Devlin greeted them and took the empty chair.

"I think you know that you were on the short list for the controller job," Mr. Frindhim said. "You've been an asset to the company since you came on, and I'm offering you the position. You'll start Monday."

The Assistant Vice President handed Devlin a folder. "Your salary goes up twenty percent. You'll have a review every ninety days to go over your progress for the quarter. You'll get an extra week of vacation, too."

"That's wonderful, thank you so much. I'm honored to accept the job," Devlin said. He wasn't just honored, he wanted to run around the building screaming like a lunatic.

"Great," Mr. Frindhim said. "My assistant will put your promotion in a company-wide email. We'll include you in the process for hiring your replacement."

"Thank you," Devlin said, standing and shaking each man's hand.

He managed to hold back the huge grin until he left the office, and then he couldn't help himself and smiled so broadly that his cheeks hurt.

"Good news, I take it?" Sam, one of his fellow accountants asked as Devlin sat at his desk.

"I got it."

"Great news! Want to go out and celebrate?"

"Yeah, I would, but my sister has a thing."

His brows rose. "A thing?"

"Yeah, she's working at a candy shop at a zoo and they're having some kind of party tonight and I promised I'd go."

"Maybe tomorrow?"

"I won't be in tomorrow, actually. Since Trina lives in New Jersey, I'm staying at a hotel for the night so I don't have to drive back late. But next week, definitely."

"Cool. Congrats, again."

"Thanks."

Devlin finished his work for the day and left, calling his parents on the way home. He'd left work early so that he could run home, change, and head down to the zoo for Trina's party.

"I'm so proud of you," his mom said at hearing the news.

"Congratulations, son."

"Thanks. I was beginning to think my five-year plan wasn't going to happen."

"You and your plans," his mom said with a chuckle. "Life wasn't meant to be planned out to the minute."

"Sorry Mom, you just don't understand because you're not a Type A personality. I like having my life planned."

"I don't know where you got that from."

"Me," his dad said. "It's what makes us Potter men so irresistible."

"Well, I don't know about that. I think it's your cute tushes."

Devlin groaned, "Mom!"

She laughed. "Are you on the way to the zoo?"

"Not yet. I have to change. I'll be there around eight."

The party started at seven, but Devlin knew he wouldn't be able to leave early enough to make it at the start.

"I'll let Trina know. See you tonight."

He said goodbye and ended the call. He stopped at his condo long enough to take a quick shower and change into jeans and a button-down shirt. He'd already packed an overnight bag, so he grabbed it and headed back to his car. Setting the GPS for the Amazing Adventures Safari Park, he turned on the radio and started the journey. He was curious about his sister's new job, working with their cousin Lexy at a candy shop in the zoo.

He and Trin were very different people, but he supposed that was the way of siblings. Where he'd excelled in school and gone on to college, Trin had been happy to get average grades in school and work retail instead. It had been her dream to work for Lexy at a bakery because Lexy was an award-winning baker. He'd always hoped that his sister would decide to go to college, but he knew that she was happy and that was what mattered. Not the degrees or the job title, but the happiness.

Which made him take pause.

Was he happy?

Hell yes! He'd just gotten the promotion he'd been chomping at the bit for. Except, there was a part of him that wished he'd had someone to see when he came home at night. He dated frequently, but he'd never found a woman that made him feel like she was the one for him. He thought there should be fireworks and instant attraction. Trina had a new boyfriend named Justus, who also worked at the zoo. Devlin hadn't met him yet, but it was his job as older brother to make sure his sister wasn't making any bad decisions, so he had a few questions for the new guy in her life.

"So," he said to himself, "if my career is on track, then maybe it's time to start looking for a relationship."

Deciding that it was a good idea, Devlin promised himself that he'd focus on finding a girlfriend and starting the next chapter of his life.

Devlin arrived at the park at eight thirty. He'd messaged Trin that he was stuck in a little traffic, and she'd promised to save him his favorite candy—dark chocolate sea salt caramels.

There were guards at the gate. They asked for ID, verifying that he was on the list of invited guests. Trina told him that the park had closed early that evening for the event.

"Follow the candlelit walkway," one of the guards said as he closed the big gate behind Devlin.

He looked around and saw a paper lantern sitting at the edge of a path. The interior flickered with candlelight.

"Thanks," he said, heading toward the lantern. More lanterns appeared every few feet that led him to a large, open area that was full of people milling about. He made his way through the crowd to the building with the sign that read, Lexy's Sweet Treasures.

He found his parents inside, said hello, and then hugged Lexy and Trina.

"It looks great," he said. "Are you excited about opening to the public?"

Lexy grinned. "Yes! I can't wait. Did you get any treats?"

He looked at Trina. "She promised to save me some chocolate."

"I did," Trina said. "Hold on."

Lexy waved to a man who joined them. "Devlin, this is my boyfriend, Win. This is my cousin, Devlin."

He shook Win's hand. "Nice to meet you. I've heard a lot about you."

"Me, too. Glad you could make it."

Trina appeared with a small glass plate with six dark chocolate squares topped with sea salt, which she handed to Devlin. Right behind her was a tall man, who looked Devlin over silently and then smiled and stuck out his hand. "You must be the brother."

He chuckled as he shook his hand. "Yes, I'm Devlin. You're the boyfriend, I take it?"

Trina said, "You guys are being weird. This is Justus."

"I heard you like math. Are you sure? Because you look like you work out for a living."

Devlin worked out often. He took pride in his well-toned body and big muscles. He also had a number of tatts, which were all hidden under his work clothes.

"Trin always said that I was a walking contradiction."

"You are!" she said. "You look like a biker or a hoodlum but you wear a suit and work with numbers all day."

"I never said that anything about me made sense," Devlin said. "But I'm happy, and that's what matters."

Trin stared up at him in silence for a moment. Then she said, "I'm happy."

Devlin glanced at Justus and saw the protective way the man stood, just behind his sister, watching for trouble. "I'm glad."

She tilted her head. "Are you really happy?"

"I got offered the promotion today."

"What? Yay! I'm so proud of you!" She laughed as she hugged him.

Something caught his attention and in the open doorway he saw a beautiful blonde woman staring at him. Her blue eyes were piercing all the way through to his heart, and he felt a tug of something familiar, as if he'd known her his whole life, even though he'd never laid eyes on her before.

"Thanks, kiddo," he said, extracting her arms from around his neck.

"What's wrong?" she asked.

"Nothing's wrong," he said, flashing her a smile. "I'll be right back."

He set the plate of chocolates down on one of the tables and stalked through the shop. The blonde took one last look at him and disappeared, but he wasn't about to let her get away. He couldn't think past how beautiful she was, and how much he wanted to talk to her. He'd never been so singularly captivated by a woman. The only thought banging around in his skull was a word he'd never uttered about a woman in his life before: MINE.

CHAPTER THREE

Jenni finished filling a large glass jar with individually wrapped watermelon taffy and carried it to the main room of the shop and set it on one of the tables. In an hour, the doors would be opened and the party would start. Every person who lived and worked in the zoo, along with Lexy and Trina's families, would have a chance to try out the goodies.

"You'll be late for the debut," Lexy said. "Go put on something comfy and come back and enjoy the night."

"It looks great," Jenni said as she untied her apron and hung it on a wooden peg inside the kitchen.

"It really does." Lexy looked around the main room, her eyes glittering with happiness. "I can't believe how fast everything came together. I don't know if I mentioned it, but thank you so much for coming to work here. I wouldn't have been able to pull this off without your help."

"I love working here. It's downright sweet."

Lexy laughed. "It sure is."

"I'll be back shortly."

"See you soon."

Jenni left the shop and hurried to the employee cafeteria, taking the hidden entrance and rushing into her house. After taking a quick shower, she stood in front of her closet and tried to decide what to wear. It wasn't as if it was a fancy event that demanded a particular type of outfit. Lexy was wearing a simple black dress with a pretty yellow belt, a color that Jenni was coming to associate with the sweet female.

Jenni's lioness growled softly in her mind and a shiver raced through her. Her beast was feeling a little anxious or excited, and she didn't know why. She didn't think she was nervous to meet Lexy and Trina's families, but maybe that was part of it. She was excited to share in the shop's debut and wanted everyone to like the taffy that she'd made.

Choosing a jean skirt that fell to mid-thigh, she paired it with a dressy green tank and a thin, white sweater that hung off one shoulder. She slipped on a pair of sandals, and then brushed her hair out, deciding to leave it long. Her eyes were bright blue, but as she stared in the mirror over her bathroom sink, she could see the faint gold of her lioness peeking through.

"What's going on with you?" she asked her reflection.

Not that she expected the beast to actually answer her, but still it would have been nice if she had a reason for the odd feeling that suddenly stole over her. Maybe something good was going to happen. Maybe her soulmate would be on one of the VIP tours that weekend.

Now that would be amazing.

Giving herself a final peek in the mirror, she headed back to the shop for the party. The park had closed early so they could enjoy themselves without worrying about park guests or working. By the time the party started, the shop was packed and so was the surrounding area, where tables and chairs had been set up.

Jenni maneuvered herself through the crowd to the shop, found Lexy and Trina, and met their families.

"I thought you had a brother?" Jenni asked Trina.

"I do. He's running late," she said.

She listened to her two human friends as their families gushed over their success, and her heart panged a little. She knew that her pride was happy for her job and would support her, but it wasn't quite the same as having actual family around to pat her on the back. She hadn't spoken to her mother in years. When she was younger, she'd tried to keep in touch, but the alpha had expertly cut Jenni out of her mother's life. She'd promised herself that she'd never choose a male over her own children, like her mother had.

She had zero plans to have a child with a male who wasn't her soulmate. Even though she was tired of being alone, she'd rather be alone than have a cub with someone who may not stick around for the long haul. Deciding that she'd taken up enough space in the shop, she snagged a grape gummy lion from a plate on one of the tables and popped it into her mouth as she walked out of the shop. She found her pride and joined them.

"We were just talking about the tours," Jupiter said. His mate, Celeste, was standing in front of him, holding a plate of chocolate covered strawberries.

"I hope more mates show up," Celeste said. "I can't believe after all the tours that only two of the new mates came from them."

"It's a good idea," Caesar said. "I think it will happen in the right time for us."

Mercer said, "I hope the right time is soon."

Jenni opened her mouth to agree with him, when she caught a faint scent on the air and it made her beast stand up and take notice. Her skin prickled and a shiver of arousal slid through her. Tilting her head, she closed her eyes and inhaled, sorting through the different scents of food and shifters, until she found the scent that intrigued her and her lioness. It was the scent of the woods at night, dark and earthy. Opening her eyes, she followed the scent back to the shop, where she stood in the doorway and located the source.

He was wearing jeans that were tight enough to highlight every muscular inch of his long legs, and a button-down shirt that was rolled at the sleeves revealing tattoos on his arms. His hair was dark and cropped short, and when he turned to face her and their eyes met, she saw a spark of interest in the baby blue depths. She'd never been more singularly attracted to a male in all her life.

Her fingers curled into the doorjamb and she was vaguely aware of the sound of cracking wood. She released her grip on the door and turned away, walking quickly from the shop. Her lioness was right under her skin and she felt like she was two seconds from shifting and trying to climb that male like a tree.

Which would have been fine, if there weren't humans who knew nothing of their natures standing in the shop. She needed to clear her head and cool her cat down. And then she could go back and find the male who intrigued her so.

"Hey," a masculine voice called to her as she turned down a path away from the shop.

A warm hand grasped her arm and she stopped, turning to face the very male she'd been trying to get a little distance from in the shop.

"Where are you going in such a hurry?" he asked.

She opened her mouth to answer, and could feel her lioness wanting to purr, so she snapped her teeth together with an audible click.

He chuckled. "Cat got your tongue?"

She laughed and felt herself relax a little. Probably because he was still holding her arm gently but firmly.

"My tongue is just fine, thanks."

He arched a brow and her cheeks heated.

"I mean, ahem, that I'm good. Do you always follow strange women to ask where they're going?"

He looked down at her. He towered over her by a foot, and his broad shoulders and muscular body seemed to strain the seams of the shirt he wore. Which, her cat assured her, would look wonderful balled up on the floor of her bedroom.

"It's not a habit. I just…thought we had a connection back there, but before I could get close, you disappeared like your ass was on fire." He peeked around her and then grinned. "Nope, it's not."

"Thanks for the concern for my ass," she said, dryly.

"I'm Devlin Potter."

"Oh! You're Trina's brother."

"Yes. I promise that at least eighty percent of what she told you about me is utter lies."

"Nothing bad, I promise. I'm Jenni Brisban."

"You work for Lexy. She mentioned you."

"I hope only good things."

"Of course."

Her lioness was banging around in her skull, assuring Jenni that this male was their soulmate. This sexy, sexy male, who maybe had more tattoos in more interesting places that needed to be explored right away.

"Fuck, you're gorgeous," he said, cupping her face. "Sweet Jenni."

His touch ignited something deep inside, and she knew then that her cat was entirely on point. Devlin was her soulmate.

Her human soulmate.

Don't care, her cat seemed to say, urging Jenni to close the distance to his utterly kissable lips and find out if he tasted as good as he smelled.

She wrapped her hands around his wrists and rose onto her toes. He lowered his head and brushed his lips over hers. Once. Twice. Then he lingered, opening his mouth and swiping his tongue over her lips. She opened her mouth with a sigh and stroked her tongue against his. Her stomach fluttered and her cat purred in her mind as he laid one large hand on the small of her back and drew her against him. She couldn't miss the hard ridge of his erection, and suddenly it was the only thing she could think about.

Except he was human. And didn't humans like to date before they had sex? Not just roll into bed at first sight.

She pulled from the kiss, her heart pounding in her chest.

"Want to get out of here?" he asked roughly, resting his forehead against hers. She could hear the rapid beating of his heart.

Although it killed her to say it, she had no choice. After one of the gorillas fell asleep at his soulmate's home during their first night together and shifted while he slept, potentially endangering them all, the council had passed a law that their people were forbidden from spending the night outside of the zoo.

It wasn't that late. She could go somewhere with him and come back later, but she knew her cat wasn't going to go for that.

"I," she started. She couldn't finish the sentence though. She didn't know what to say. Then she had an idea. "I can't leave, but we can go somewhere private."

"Your place? Wouldn't that be the same as leaving?"

"No, there are some apartments on the property. We can hang out for a bit in private and then come back to the party. Unless you don't want to? You came to see your sister."

"Yeah, I did. But I want to see you now. I can't explain why I feel so drawn to you, but you're irresistible. Just a taste and I want more."

Warmth pooled in her belly.

She took his hand and they walked down the path together. She hadn't planned it, but she'd been on her way to the apartments before he stopped her. Her cat must be psychic. The apartments were in a converted barn which had at one time been part of a petting zoo. After the human mates came along, they needed a way to live at the zoo without drawing suspicion from their families. Inside the barn were three apartments. Only one apartment had been finished entirely and was furnished and had electricity and plumbing. The other two were facades. Lexy and Trina had both told their parents they were living in the apartments, so Jenni knew she couldn't take Devlin into the finished apartment, but there was a gathering area outside of the apartments with several couches, which would be perfect for getting to know her soulmate.

"What do you do?" she asked.

"I actually just got promoted today to be my company's controller. I work for an accounting firm."

"Congratulations. I have no idea what a controller does, though. I'm guessing...math?"

He laughed. "Yep. I'll handle things like the company's budget, financial reporting, and some salary aspects. I was the assistant controller before, so I was waiting for the job to open up. I'm sure it sounds boring."

"Not at all. I'm just not much of a math person. Thank goodness for the calculator on the phone."

He squeezed her hand lightly as he chuckled. "Do you like making candy?"

"I do. I used to work in the security office. I just wanted to do something different."

"I get that. My family thought I would go into professional body building or own a gym or be a trainer. I like working out, I just don't want to do it for a career."

She grasped his bicep and gave it a squeeze. Her ovaries cheered at how rock solid he was. "I can tell you like to work out."

They reached the barn, and she entered the code to unlock the front door. He followed her in and she shut the door. Flipping on one of the light switches at the side of the door, she illuminated the gathering area. A portion of the barn had been left open, and beyond that were the three apartments, which looked like two-story condos.

"Do you live here?" he asked.

"No. The apartments are for some of our staff. I live off-site." She cringed at the lie, but hid it by clearing her throat. "I thought we could hang out and get to know each other without leaving the park."

"Sure," he said, leading her to one of the couches. He sat down and she joined him.

Before she could get settled on the comfortable cushion, he hauled her onto his lap, her knees straddling him. She squeaked in surprise and then gasped as his hands settled on the outside of her thighs. She settled her hands on his shoulders and looked down at him, captivated by the glittering interest in his eyes. They'd darkened from pale blue to navy.

"Tell me that you feel it, too," he whispered, nipping at her chin. "Tell me you want me as much as I want you. Not just for tonight, but for every night."

Her cat yowled in happiness.

She pressed one hand to his cheek and sank the fingers of her other hand into his hair. "I do."

"Come home with me," he said, his voice tipping low.

"I can't. Not tonight."

She pressed her lips to his and he opened immediately to

her tongue, sucking on it as he slowly pushed her skirt up her thighs. She fisted his hair, tilting his head to deepen the kiss, sliding her tongue against his and trying to stifle the purr from her cat. He slid the skirt up to her waist and then spread his fingers across her panties.

Easing from the kiss, she unbuttoned his shirt and spread it open, gazing in rapture at all his sexy muscles. His pecs flexed under her gaze and she smiled.

"You're so sexy," she said.

"Oh? I'm not the only one," he said.

He curled his fingers around the edge of her panties and pulled them to the side and then he slid his fingers down to her pussy. She gasped as he slid one finger into her heat.

"Lift your shirt," he demanded.

She grasped the hem of her top and drew it up her body, shuddering as he slid his finger out and pushed it in again. She caught the center of her bra and lifted it too, until she bared herself for him. She leaned forward and kissed him, gasping as he pushed a second finger into her. He lowered his head to her breast, sucking her nipple slowly into his mouth. She arched her back as he moved to her other nipple and sucked it into his mouth with the same slow movements.

Reaching between them, she straightened and grasped his belt, undoing the buckle and sliding it apart. Tugging the button open and zipper down, she slid her hand under his jeans and boxers and wrapped her hand around his thick length. He flexed his hips as he released her nipple.

"Fuck, Jenni."

"More," she said, pushing at her cat to keep the purr from her voice.

He pulled his hands away and arched under her, shoving his jeans and boxers past his hips and freeing his erection. Then he pushed her skirt up to her waist and pulled her panties to the side, exposing her pussy.

He looked at her, his gaze searching. "Your eyes are so beautiful."

She smiled and gripped his cock firmly. She pressed it to her entrance and lowered herself down on him slowly. Letting go of his cock, she linked her hands at the back of his neck and let out a gusty groan as he surged up and buried himself entirely within her.

He grasped her hips and lifted her almost entirely off him, and then lowered her. She relaxed into his hold and pressed her cheek against his, loving the way that he felt inside her. Just as quickly as he'd begun to move them together, he let go of his grip on her, and placed his hand on her abdomen and grazed her clit with his thumb. She gasped and he tightened his hand on her hip, keeping her in place.

He rubbed her clit, up and down at first and then side to side, until her breath caught when he rubbed one side and she knew he'd found her sweet spot. He played his thumb against that spot, rubbing fast and then slow, alternating until she was panting hard and shivering.

"Devlin," she moaned.

"Come for me, sweet thing," he whispered in her ear.

He rubbed her clit faster and she threw back her head as her toes curled and the center of her body turned to molten liquid. She cried out, biting her lip against the roar that threatened to break free as her climax thundered through her. Devlin grabbed her hips with both hands and began to fuck her, moving her hard and fast on his cock, prolonging her climax until it seemed like an endless wave of pleasure. His fingers dug into her flesh as he came, spasming inside her.

Just as she thought she couldn't be any happier, he kissed her neck and gave her a gentle nip. It wasn't like a real marking. He didn't have fangs, like a male shifter would. But all the same, she fell a little bit in love with her soulmate right then.

"You are perfect, Jenni," he said with a rough voice, "every inch of you."

"You're very sweet. And perfect, too." She rested her cheek on his shoulder, content to be in his arms for however long they could manage.

After several quiet minutes, he hugged her a little tighter and said, "I want to take you back to the hotel with me. Stay the night with me, Jenni."

How she wanted to, but she knew she couldn't.

She sat up and kissed him. "I can't."

He let out a short growl, which was adorable. "Tomorrow?"

"I have to work, of course. But after, I'm free."

"I'll pick you up."

She shook her head. It would be easier to get home if she drove herself. "I'll meet you for dinner."

He wiggled under her and pulled his phone from his back pocket. "Are you really going to let me see you again?"

She blinked in surprise. "What?"

He fiddled with the phone and said, "I mean, I'm trying to take you home and rock your world in a real bed, and you won't even let me pick you up tomorrow. Are you secretly married?"

With a snort, she started to laugh and shook her head. "I promise. Let me come to you, okay?"

He turned the phone to face her and she saw that he'd made a contact for her. She entered her cell number and then texted herself so when she got back to her place she'd have his number, too. He dropped the phone to the couch and cupped her face, drawing her close and kissing her. She could have stayed there with him for hours, but she knew she needed to get back to the party. She wasn't even sure how long they'd been gone and was glad that no one had come looking for her.

"Ok," he said. "I guess we should get back, even though I don't want our time together to end."

"Me, either."

She slipped from his lap and straightened her clothes. She knew that every shifter in the zoo would be able to smell him on her skin, but she was proud to have such a strong male for a mate. Now, though, she had to deal with the fact that her mate was human and she couldn't just come right out and tell him the truth of her shifter abilities. She needed to talk to Caesar and get his advice. Most likely, he would tell her to take her time and not tell Devlin until they were in love, and with the new law forbidding unmated shifters from staying out of the park overnight, she wouldn't be able to know what it was like to wake up in her mate's arms for...however long it took.

She stifled a deep sigh that welled inside her. It was easier for shifters because they could be trusted to keep the secret. But with a human mate, the shifter had to be cautious not to share the secret too early. She didn't like not telling Devlin, but she knew it wasn't the right time.

He stood and tucked himself back into his jeans, and then she watched him button his shirt. It was a shame to cover up all that glorious, sexy skin.

"I like your tattoos," she said. "I was just wondering if there are many tattooed finance guys out there."

He grinned. Damn, he was gorgeous.

"I keep my sleeves rolled down so the tattoos aren't visible. I suppose there are some visibly tattooed finance people, but for me the tattoos are personal and not relevant to my business life."

She liked them. They were sexy.

He drew close and pressed his lips to hers for an all-too-brief moment. "Are you sure I can't convince you to come back to the hotel with me?"

She pressed her lips into a thin line and mentally shoved her eager lioness. "Another time, maybe."

"I have to go back to Rhode Island on Sunday."

She'd known from Trina that he didn't live in New Jersey, but the idea that he was several states away hit her suddenly and she wanted to grab hold of him and never let go. It would be difficult to get to know him if he was so far away.

"We have the weekend, though," she pointed out.

He half-smiled. "A hundred weekends wouldn't be enough."

She went onto her toes and kissed him. "Let's get back to the party."

"Right," he said, exhaling sharply. "Lexy saved me some of my favorite dark chocolate caramels with sea salt."

"Oh, I like those! But my favorite candy is peanut butter cups."

They left the building, and she was happy to see that no one had come looking for her. Not that she would have cared if anyone in her pride knew she'd had sex in the barn, but she didn't want to deal with them just yet. They still had time that night to get to know each other.

Not nearly enough time, though.

CHAPTER FOUR

Devlin had been unable to sleep, spending most of Thursday night tossing and turning. His skin still smelled like Jenni. A sweet and wild scent that reminded him of jasmine and thunderstorms. He'd hated leaving the park and had lingered as long as he could to spend time with the irresistible woman. He'd never been so thoroughly enchanted with anyone before, but he was bespelled by Jenni.

Which had its own problems, chief among them that he didn't live in New Jersey. He had three days with her and then he was back to Rhode Island and his promotion. Oddly enough, the job that had meant everything to him now paled in comparison to how he felt about her, even after just a few hours together. It was crazy to think about walking away from his job and moving to New Jersey for a woman he'd met less than twenty-four hours ago, but that was exactly what his heart was telling him to do.

The last time he'd been in a serious relationship, things had fallen apart because he'd been busy with school and work and had neglected his girlfriend. He couldn't even think about treating Jenni like that. He'd hate to work nights and weekends, letting his job—which had at one time been everything to him—ruin things with Jenni.

After he'd been in bed for a couple hours last night without being able to sleep, he'd gone down to the twenty-four-hour gym and lifted weights, hoping to tire himself out, but it hadn't put a dent in the insomnia that not having Jenni with him caused.

Sitting up with a groan, Devlin rubbed his eyes with the heels of his hands and mentally smacked himself. He was running head first into a future that he wasn't sure Jenni even wanted. If she'd wanted to start something serious with him, he would have thought she'd come back to the hotel with him so they could spend the night together, but she'd been adamant that she couldn't. Their time in the apartment building had been hot as hell. She made the sweetest sound when she fell apart, and her body had positively glowed after her climax. He was even certain that her eyes had changed from blue to gold, but after their time together they were blue again and he wasn't sure he hadn't imagined the change.

His phone chirped and he saw a text from his mom asking if he was joining them in the hotel restaurant for breakfast. He wasn't in the mood to eat. All he wanted to do was go to the park and find Jenni, but she was working and he knew that wasn't appropriate.

Answering that he'd be down shortly, he walked into the bathroom and turned on the shower. Images of the time with Jenni in his arms flashed through his mind and his body sprang to life. It was going to be a damn long day if he walked around with a hard-on the whole time. He showered and dressed in jeans and a t-shirt, and headed down to the restaurant where his parents were already at the buffet loading their plates with breakfast items.

He checked in with the hostess and picked up a plate and filled it with scrambled eggs and toasted a whole wheat bagel, before joining his parents at their table. A waitress came over and filled his coffee mug, and he added a spoon of sugar and then took a sip.

"How did you sleep?" his mom asked.

He grunted.

"That good, huh?" his dad asked with a chuckle.

"Oh, I bet you wished you'd had more time with your little friend."

"Mom, geez," he chided.

She grinned. "Just teasing, sweetheart. She was quite the smitten kitten."

His brows lifted. "Do you think so?"

"Of course. She couldn't keep her eyes off you all night. Did you meet her family?" his mom said.

He shook his head. "Her mom lives somewhere else, and she doesn't know her dad. She said she lives in a development with her friends, and Caesar took her in after her mom left. She thinks of him like a dad and his sons like brothers. Her and her friends run the security for the park, except that she started working for Lexy a little while ago."

"That's so sad she doesn't know her father," his mom said. "You and Trina were very lucky to have such a great dad."

"I think so, too," his dad said.

"You're a great dad," Devlin said.

"So, you like her," his dad said.

"Yeah. I really do. It's complicated, though."

"Love always is," his mom said.

"Especially," his dad said, "if you're already thinking about the future, which I think you might be."

Devlin nodded. "I never thought I'd meet a woman and immediately be able to picture the house and white picket fence and kids. It's crazy fast, but it feels right."

His mom smiled. "What's complicated about it, then?"

"She lives in New Jersey and I don't."

She shrugged. "So, fix that."

"What, ask her to move to Rhode Island the day after meeting me?" Even though it seemed impossible, he wanted that. Wanted her to be with him so they could be together. "But she likes her life here."

"It's early, though. She might change her mind—or you might," his dad said as he picked up a piece of bacon from his plate.

"Change my mind about what?"

"Living in Rhode Island."

He settled back in his chair and hooked his arm over the chair next to him. His parents were eating their meals as if they hadn't just suggested he chuck his whole career in the toilet because he happened to meet the woman of his dreams in a zoo on a random Thursday night.

"Seriously?" he asked.

His dad looked up at him, his forkful of hashbrowns halfway to his mouth. "I know all about your five-year-plan, son. I'm just saying that you could chase your career dreams anywhere. And you work a helluva lot. It would be hard on a new relationship to be in the demanding job you're in right now."

His mom jumped in. "We're not saying walk away, we're just saying maybe be open to the idea of your life going in a different direction. It worked for us."

His dad had been an architect in New York when they were married. The hours had been terrible and she'd been lonely. He took a job in Rhode Island with a small architecture company. The pay had been less, but he'd had more time for their marriage and family.

"I never regretted that step down," he said. "I was on track to become partner. It would have meant a boatload of money for the family and success for me, but I hated coming home late at night and seeing dinner on the table, your mom asleep because she couldn't stay up long enough to greet me."

Devlin shook his head. "I don't think I can walk away from my job. I've worked so hard to get to this place."

"I'm sure she'd be willing to move. You've only just met, anyway. Give it some time and see where your future takes you," his mom said.

He wanted his future to take him directly to Jenni, and he couldn't bring himself to care whether it was Rhode Island or New Jersey, or somewhere else entirely. After only a few hours together, he already wanted to spend the rest of his life with her, and part of him was really scared by those feelings.

∾

Devlin opened the delivery containers and began to separate the meals onto the paper plates that the restaurant had included in the bags. He wasn't much of a cook, unless you counted protein shakes which he made for himself every morning. And he didn't think that Jenni would be impressed with his blender skills. So, he'd ordered dinner from a local place and also picked up a good bottle of wine and candles to make the hotel room more intimate feeling.

He texted Jenni after breakfast and hadn't expected to hear from her until her break, but she'd responded right away. It had kind of floored him how much he enjoyed getting the text from her, and when she said she would be at his hotel at seven, he'd been over the moon with excitement for their date. His original plan had been to take her to dinner, but when he'd called to make reservations at the local hot spots, everything was booked, so he'd done the next best thing—made a restaurant just for them. It was far more intimate, and he'd be lying if he said it hadn't crossed his mind that the bed was just a few feet from where they'd be eating. He'd had a taste of her and it hadn't been enough by a long shot.

There was a knock at the door as he finished lighting the candles. He blew out the match and set the book aside, brushed his suddenly sweating hands on his trousers, and walked to the door. Pulling it open, he knew his jaw hit the floor because of the gorgeous woman in front of him. Jenni wore a short black dress and heels. The dress hugged her curves and made him want to slaughter every guy who laid eyes on her.

He grabbed her around the waist and drew her into the room, kissing her as he let the door slam. She pressed her body against him, her hands linking at the back of his neck as their tongues touched and teased, and every inch of him was ready to take her right there in the middle of the room.

Putting the brakes on his libido, he pulled from the drugging kiss.

"Hi," he said.

She smiled, her lips swollen from their kiss and her eyes glittering with humor. "Hi yourself."

"I wanted to take you somewhere nice for dinner, but everywhere was booked, so I brought dinner here. If that's okay."

Her gaze flitted to the bed and then the coffee table.

"It's wonderful. I've never had anyone do this kind of thing for me."

"I'm happy to be the first one to treat you right."

He led her to the couch and sat next to her.

"I have bottled water if you don't like wine, but this is a favorite of mine and it goes great with Italian food."

"I don't know anything about wine, but I'd love to have a glass."

He poured a glass for her. "I don't know much. I go by

what I like, and not what the label says."

He filled his glass and set the wine on the table.

"Should we toast?" she asked. "Or is that only for champagne?"

"I think people can toast with whatever they'd like. What should we toast to?"

She chewed on her bottom lip in thought and then said, "The park."

"The park? Why?"

"Because it brought you to me."

Immediately, he thought of his job. And then he thought of Jenni, and how much he'd missed her all damn day. The hours dragged as if someone had attached weights to them. Without the park, he'd never have met her. But he *had* met her. And she clearly liked him if she was suggesting that he was 'brought' to her. If he believed in fate, he'd think that they were made for each other.

And maybe they were.

"To the park," he said, pushing away all thoughts of his job and concentrating on the beautiful woman before him. She deserved every ounce of his attention. He'd think about the future tomorrow.

Their glasses clinked, and they both took drinks and set their glasses on the table. He picked up the plate he'd arranged for her, of chicken marsala with egg noodles and roasted carrots. She took it and set it on her lap with a smile, lifting the knife and fork from the table.

"It looks delicious."

"I wasn't sure what you'd like and I didn't want to ruin the fact that I hadn't been able to get a reservation anywhere."

"I don't mind. It's nice to just have the two of us. And I love chicken marsala."

He put his plate on his lap and cut into the chicken,

taking a bite of the tender, slightly tangy meat and noodles. His gaze flew to her face when she groaned happily, the sound traveling straight to his cock, which had gone shamelessly hard the moment he'd seen her.

"Wow, this is really good."

"I'm glad you like it."

While they ate, he asked about working at the park and discovered that she'd been working there since she was a teenager and had always worked security.

"Why security?" he asked.

She shrugged. "It's what my... family does."

The pause had been significant, and he wondered if she had struggled to find a word to describe her friends. He had friends, but none close enough that he'd call them family. He thought it was great that she'd found such a supportive group after having been abandoned by her mother.

"Are you happy now that you're at the sweets shop?"

"I really love it."

"How was the first day?"

"So cool. We had lots of patrons come in, and there were people who remembered when the shop was open years ago before the couple retired."

"Lexy always dreamed of opening her own place. She and Trina planned to work together since they were kids. It's awesome to see them both happy, and I'm glad you had a great first day."

"What did you do today?"

"Missed you."

"Really?"

"Hell yes." He paused and then asked, "Did you miss me?"

Not for the first time, a bolt of uncertainty spiked through him. What if he was the only one feeling the strong attraction between them?

"Of course, I did." Her brow drew down and she said, "I hardly slept at all last night."

"Me, too."

She put her empty plate on the coffee table and he set his down next to it. He reached for her hand and linked their fingers. He wanted to say a hundred things, but all thought fled when she moved to him and kissed him. She was on her knees on the couch, her fingers tunneling into his hair as she licked the seam of his mouth. He opened immediately, his hands going to her waist and pulling her closer. He lifted her against him and stood, walking to the bed and slowly lowering her. She gave him a wicked smile and rolled away, rising onto her knees in the center of the bed.

"You have on too many clothes to get on this bed," she said, reaching for the zipper at the back of her dress. The sound of it lowering made his brain fog over as he watched her slowly strip, lifting the dress up her thighs, revealing the black satin panties that covered his most favorite place, and the sweet indentation of her navel. The bra matched the panties, and he grinned as she tossed the dress from the bed.

He undid his tie, fighting the desire to growl. He'd never felt so primal, but there was something about his sexy sweetheart that brought out that feeling in him. Stripping from his shirt, he kicked off his shoes and dropped his trousers. He pushed them off his legs and tugged his socks off, before he rested his fingertips on the waistband of his boxer briefs.

"These, too, sweetheart?"

She licked her lips and nodded.

"Take off your bra first."

She nibbled on her bottom lip as she reached behind her back to undo the clasp of her bra. It loosened and she drew it slowly down her arms, tossing it in the same direction as her dress.

"Let me see you," she said, her voice taking on a sexy, low tone.

He took his time lowering his boxers, until he could drop them down his legs. He straightened and wrapped his hand around his cock, giving it a pump. "Been hard all day for you, sweetheart."

"Come up here," she said.

He climbed onto the bed on his knees and joined her. He cupped her breasts, loving the warm softness of her skin. Her nipples were hard and begging to be sucked. She wrapped her hand around his cock and gazed up at him as she began to stroke him from root to tip.

"You were on my mind all day. Your muscles, your sexy smile, your beautiful eyes. Every inch of you."

He groaned as she pumped him faster, and knew it wouldn't take much to send him over the edge. He'd been dancing on it since they'd parted the night before.

He kissed her and grasped her wrist, stopping her motions. She made a mewling sound of protest and then she moaned as he pushed her panties down her hips and slid his middle finger between her pussy lips. She was so hot and wet that his brain threatened to stall out at just how sexy she was. Instead, he curled a finger into her pussy and slowly began to stroke into her depths. She grasped his shoulders, kissing him more fervently, as he settled his thumb on her clit and began to play with it. He added a second finger, rubbing them along her inner walls as his thumb worked fast circles around her clit.

She broke the kiss, panting heavily and leaning against him as he worked her to climax. She spread her thighs further apart as her pussy began to clutch his fingers.

"Devlin, Devlin," she chanted his name breathlessly.

He felt her pussy contract hard just before she cried out in pleasure. He lifted his fingers from her and sucked them into his mouth, groaning at the sweet taste of her pleasure. Pushing her to her back, he tugged her panties from her legs and spread her thighs, lowering his head and licking her cream. She moaned loudly and fisted his hair, lifting her hips and holding him against her as he devoured her, lapping at her liquid heat.

He kissed her clit and flicked it with his tongue until she gasped and writhed under him. Planting kisses up the center of her body, he grinned when he rose over her, his cock probing her entrance. Her legs went around his waist and she crossed her ankles at his lower back.

He locked his gaze with hers as he pushed into her wet heat slowly. She was the hottest, tightest heaven he'd ever had the pleasure of touching. In that moment, when their bodies were connected in the most primal of ways, he was hers. Entirely.

Sliding from her channel, he pushed back in with a groan. He clenched his teeth, knowing that she felt too good and he was too on-edge to last long. She laid her hand on his cheek and lifted her head to kiss him. Dropping her head to the bed, she moaned and began to meet his thrusts with her own, her heels digging into his ass as she urged him on.

They moved together, bodies slick with sweat. He felt his orgasm tingling at the base of his spine and he knew he was done for. She just felt too good. Gripping her shoulders, he drove himself into her, pulling her hard against him and fucking her soundly until he came, her name on his lips. She sighed sweetly and he rested his head on her shoulder as he caught his breath. He shuddered, his cock softening and slipping from her depths. Easing to the side, he hugged her close and kissed her shoulder, her neck and her cheek.

"You're wonderful," he murmured.

"You are, too."

"Stay with me tonight, Jenni."

"I can't. But I can stay a while. I'm not ready to say goodbye yet."

He wanted to beg her to stay, but he didn't want to push her. Deciding he'd take what he could get, he kissed her throat. "I'm not ready, either."

CHAPTER FIVE

A loud banging woke Jenni from a sound sleep. At first, she thought she'd dreamed the noise, but then it happened again. She sat up and rubbed her eyes, and realized immediately that she wasn't in her home under the park. She was in the hotel!

"Jenni Brisban, open this fucking door immediately," Caesar said, his voice a loud growl through the door.

"Shit!" She gasped and hurried from the bed, scrambling to find her dress and pull it over her head.

"What the fuck is going on? Who is that?" Devlin demanded as he turned on the nightstand lamp and got out of bed.

"It's Caesar. I wasn't supposed to stay here tonight, but I fell asleep. Damn it!"

"How did he know you were here?" Devlin pulled his trousers on and headed for the door.

She grabbed his arm but he twisted from her grip and went to the door, slamming the security bar open and twisting the handle. He pulled the door open and said, "Do you have any idea how loud you are? We were asleep."

Jenni stood in the center of the room, her bra, panties, and heels clutched to her chest, and her cheeks hot with blush.

"I'm sorry, Caesar."

Devlin shot her a sharp look. "What are you sorry for? We're consenting adults. There isn't anything wrong with what we did."

"You don't know anything about our people," Caesar said.

Behind him, Jenni saw Jupiter and Xavier. They wore expressions that were identical to Caesar, a mixture of worry and displeasure. Before she'd left to meet Devlin, she'd sworn to Caesar that she'd return to the park before midnight. She had zero memory of falling asleep with Devlin, but she shouldn't have trusted herself. Her plan had been to only make love to him once and then leave, but they'd been naked and holding each other after the first time, and she'd been unable to go anywhere but back to the heavens.

"Look," Devlin said, stepping into the center of the doorway so she couldn't leave without pushing him aside. "I don't appreciate you storming over here like Jenni's some wayward child. She came here of her own free will. You should respect that."

Jenni could tell that Caesar was walking a fine line of fury, and although she was proud that Devlin was standing up for her, and definitely a little turned on by his aggressive stance, she'd messed up and had to be accountable for it.

Putting her hand on Devlin's shoulder, she said to Caesar, "Let me say goodbye."

"Jenni," Devlin said. She put her finger on his lips and he narrowed his eyes but didn't say anything else.

"Be quick," Caesar said.

She pulled Devlin back into the room, even though with their superior hearing every male would know exactly what she said. "I'm sorry I have to leave like this. I promised I wouldn't stay the night."

"Why does it matter? Why can't you stay here?"

She wanted to cry or yell about the unfairness of the situation, but it wouldn't fix anything. "Because I can't, Devlin, I'm sorry. There are things about me that I can't share with you right now."

He crossed his arms over his chest and looked down at her. She was surprised by the abrupt coldness she saw. "I won't try to guilt you into staying."

Her eyes stung with tears and her mouth went salty. "Devlin."

"Go on, Jenni. Your *friends* need you, apparently more than you need me."

She saw him shut down. Saw the moment that he shuttered his feelings, and her lioness roared in dismay. She pulled open the door and looked at Caesar pleadingly, but he shook his head. He put his big hand on the door to hold it open, and the nearly imperceptible growl she heard from him told her that her time was up.

She grabbed her purse from the couch and looked at Devlin. "I'm sorry," she said, knowing that the words were utterly, pathetically useless.

He didn't answer her, but she hadn't really expected him to. She left the room, hugging her purse to her chest. The door shut with a bang that made her heart clench in grief. It sounded like a coffin lid closing. A terrible sort of final sound. Not the beginning of something, but the sad, awful ending of it. Handing the park's SUV keys to Jupiter, she hung her head and followed her alpha out of the hotel. Her lioness was wrecked, anxious to go back to the room and tell Devlin everything—what she was, why she couldn't stay outside of the zoo. But there was no way that Caesar would allow her to do that in public, let alone with a male who had just shut her down so coldly.

She climbed into the second row of the other SUV. Xavier drove and Caesar sat in the passenger seat, while Jupiter drove the other SUV behind them.

"I'm sorry I messed up," she said, trying not to fall into a weeping ball.

Caesar was silent for a long moment, and she wondered if he was pondering her punishment. She'd broken a rule, and even though Devlin was her soulmate, rules were meant to be followed for the safety of them all, and she couldn't go breaking the rules willy-nilly.

"You scared the fuck out of us," he said. "If it weren't for the trackers on the GPS, we wouldn't have known where you were. It was foolish to meet him at the hotel."

"I hadn't planned to stay."

"But you did."

"What's going to happen to me?"

He turned and looked at her. "You told me earlier that he's your soulmate. Are you certain?"

"Yes."

He blew out a breath. "This is getting more and more difficult."

"What is?" she asked.

"Soulmates. Earlier I would have suggested that you could bring him to the park to reveal your nature to him, the way that Justus revealed his bear to Trina. But the male that we left in that hotel room is pissed six ways from Sunday, and I won't allow you to reveal yourself to him until you're certain he's not walking away."

Her heart panged. "I think he wanted me to fight to stay with him."

"But you knew you couldn't," Xavier said. "Which makes

what happened tonight something that shouldn't have. You should have been more careful, Jen, plain and simple."

"I'll be sure to remind you of those words when you get all twisted up meeting your soulmate," she muttered.

With a snort he said, "You do that."

"Am I in trouble?"

"Yes. You're in your shift in the paddocks this weekend. I don't care that you have found your soulmate, we need to be in our shifts and put on a good tour, whether they're VIPs or regular park patrons. You're unable to leave the park for twenty-four hours."

She opened her mouth to protest that Devlin was only going to be in town until Sunday night, but she snapped it shut with a click, knowing that arguing wouldn't do any good. Once Caesar made up his mind, that was it.

"Fine."

She stared out the window, her mind turning as she tried to figure out how to fix things with Devlin. He was angry, and she didn't blame him. They'd shared an amazing night. Even though she hadn't planned to fall asleep, it had felt so good to be in his arms, snuggled up in the dark. She wanted all her nights to be with him, but aside from the glaring fact he was human, he also had a job and a promotion waiting for him on Monday, several states north. She hadn't been willing to stand up to Caesar to spend the night with him, and she wondered if he'd even considered leaving his job for her.

Probably not after what happened.

She hated to admit it, but having a human mate was trickier than she'd anticipated, and she was afraid—deeply, truly afraid—that she'd lost him forever, and she'd only just gotten him.

~

Jenni lifted her phone from the apron pocket to check for an answer to her many texts and phone calls to Devlin, but the screen was blank. Every time she looked and saw that he was ignoring her, it was like a hot knife in her heart.

"I can't believe he's not returning your calls," Trina said, coming to stand next to Jenni at the counter. Jenni was bagging taffy in half-pound decorative bags to put on the shelves in the main room. She'd barely been able to concentrate on watching the scale and printing out the labels. All she could think about was that she was losing Devlin.

"What if he went back home already?"

"He's still at the hotel. I talked to our parents and they said he's holed up in his room and refuses to come out."

Jenni blinked at the tears that stung her eyes and gave Trina a watery smile. "I guess it's a good sign that he didn't leave."

"Yeah. He's just mad. Men are... well, they're idiots," Lexy said, joining them. "Devlin probably expected you to stand by him, but it's because he doesn't understand things, and he's taking it personally."

"Do you want us to go talk to him?" Trina asked.

Jenni shook her head. "No. I'm reaching out and he's rebuffing me. If he wants to be like that, then it's on him."

"Oh, honey," Lexy said, giving her a light hug. "I'm sorry he's being an ass."

"Well, that's nothing new," Trina said.

Jenni gave Trina a half-smile for the attempt at humor. "He's mine. If he walks, then I'll just be alone."

"It'll be okay," Trina said, stepping to her other side and making it a three-way-hug.

Jenni wanted to believe it, but she wasn't so sure. Her lioness snarled unhappily, and she turned her attention back to the taffy and tried to put thoughts of her soulmate from her mind.

By the time she needed to leave to get ready for the VIP tours, she'd found it nearly impossible to put Devlin out of her mind. He was firmly entrenched and under her skin, and no matter what she tried to think about, it always came back to him. Which was heaven and hell at the same time.

"I'm gonna go," she said, as she finished tying curling ribbon on a gift basket she'd created to put in the shop with a variety of sweets.

"Thanks for today. I hope you feel better," Lexy said.

"He'll come around," Trina said, smiling hopefully.

Jenni hung up her apron and nodded. "See you tomorrow."

She walked out of the shop and followed the path to the employee cafeteria, where she opened one of the commercial refrigerators and grabbed a plastic container of sliced apples with a cup of peanut butter. She dipped the slices into the peanut butter, eating as she wound her way down to their private area, and then up into the lions' paddock. She came out of the hidden entrance in the floor and popped the last peanut-butter-laden slice into her mouth. Caesar was in the shed, and so were Mercer and Justus.

Mercer gave her a one-armed hug. "You okay?"

"I'll be fine."

"Did he call you today or try to come see you?" Caesar asked.

She shook her head.

"Human males are idiots," Justus said. "He should have come for you and demanded to see you immediately. It's what I would have done."

"Yeah, but that's the point, right?" Mercer said. "He's human and they don't do things like we do. He probably thinks Jenni chose us over him and he's all butt-hurt about it."

"Shit, guys," she said, tossing the empty container into a

nearby trash receptacle. "Can we talk about anything besides my love life?"

"Sorry," Mercer said, giving her an apologetic smile.

Caesar glanced at his watch and said, "We need to shift, the first tour will start soon."

She stripped and shifted, wanting to get out of the shed and into the open space of their paddock, which had been created to mimic the Sahara. She knew exactly where she wanted to go—straight to her favorite rock for a nap, and then seeing if there were any tasty rabbits or small rodents she could chase for fun.

Caesar tapped her nose. "You have to be visible to the tours, even if you've found your soulmate. No laying on the rock all afternoon."

She let out a gruff sigh and grumbled at him, which just made him smile.

"I love you, Jenni. You're like a daughter to me, and I just want you to be safe. I want that for all of us."

She nodded and bumped his knee with her head. He held open the shed door for her and she padded out, ignoring the desire to head right for her napping spot. Behind her, Justus and Mercer came, and then Caesar. She stretched, sinking her claws into the dirt and flicking her tail, and then she joined them.

It was going to be a long day.

CHAPTER SIX

Devlin stared down at his suitcase on the bed. He'd been attempting to pack all afternoon, but he hadn't gotten very far. He wanted to leave. To go back to Rhode Island and forget about the striking blonde with curves for days. But he was too torn up to walk away. Leaving would hurt but staying hurt, too. She'd been calling and texting him, but he hadn't answered, which was a super chicken-shit way to act. He hadn't wanted to hear any excuses for why she'd chosen her friends over him, because he'd known the moment she dressed so hurriedly when they were woken up that she was going to leave with them. He knew they'd just met, but still... she hadn't put up any kind of fight at all. Not a single protest had left her mouth when Caesar said it was time to go, she'd only uttered apologies.

He deserved a hell of a lot more than apologies, that was for damn sure.

And maybe it had cut him so deeply because part of him had hoped she'd want to move up with him so he wouldn't have to make the choice to leave his job. When she'd picked them over him, he'd known immediately that she wouldn't be moving anywhere, which put the ball firmly in his court. If he wanted Jenni, he was the one that would have to quit his job and move.

He dropped his dress shoes into the suitcase and sat on the bed with a sigh. He did want her. Which was the problem and the solution at the same time. Staying with Jenni this weekend would have been easy, but come Sunday night he'd have to go and deal with his job, and that came down to a simple question—would he take the job or would he resign. Right now, he was torn in two with the question.

He looked at his phone on the dresser. He *should* call her, but he felt like a gigantic asshat and the truth was that he just didn't know what he was going to say to her.

There was a knock on the door. His heart rate kicked up and he wondered if she'd come for him. Then he heard his sister's voice through the door and his shoulders slumped.

"Open the door this instant, Devlin!"

"Go. Away."

"No! We need to talk. Open the damn door."

He stood and walked to the door, resting his hand on the knob and looking through the peephole. Which Trina had obviously covered with her finger. Typical.

"Who is 'we'?"

"Me and Lex. And our boyfriends. Now you're making a scene, so open the door."

He flipped the security bar and opened the door, finding Trina, Justus, Lexy, and Win in the hallway. "I'm not the one who's making a scene."

Trina sniffed. "You're *making* me make a scene, which is a lot worse than actually making a scene."

"You're ridiculous."

He stepped aside and the group trooped in, the guys going to the window and standing, and the girls sitting on the couch. He shut the door and joined them, sitting on a chair that faced the couch. "What can I do for you, sweet sister of mine?"

Trina rolled her eyes. "You know why I'm here. Why aren't you answering any of Jenni's calls? She was a wreck today and it's entirely your fault."

He stared at his sister, and then Lexy, letting his gaze ping to the guys. "You know that Caesar and two others came for her last night, right?"

Trina looked at Justus and he shook his head just slightly as if in warning. She sighed. "Look, Caesar is like a father to Jenni. And like any family, they have rules. And one of those rules is that they have to be back home at night. When she didn't come home, Caesar was worried."

"She's an adult."

"It's a family rule," Win said. "I've known Caesar for a long time and he cares about Jenni very deeply and doesn't want her to get hurt. Think of it like a curfew. She broke it, and he had to be sure that she was okay."

"You think I can't keep her safe?" He stood abruptly.

Win put his hands up. "Your relationship is very new. Of course, her family would want to make sure she was making good choices."

He snorted at the word "relationship." They hadn't talked about the future at all, and maybe that had been part of his plan to just take things easy until he absolutely had to talk about it, hoping that she'd be the one to bring up the distance between their homes and offer to just hop in his car and leave with him.

"There are things about Jenni that you don't know," Lexy said.

Win made an odd sound that reminded Devlin of a warning growl, like their old family German Shepherd used to make. Devlin's gaze snapped to him and he cleared his throat and said, "What Lexy means is that the girls would like you to come to the park and see Jenni."

Lexy stood. "It's important, Dev. Please? Don't pack your bag and disappear, or I promise that you're going to regret it for the rest of your life. Something bigger than your giant ego is going on here, and you need to put your injured feelings aside for a minute and come with us."

"My ego is not giant."

"It's enormous," Trina quipped, standing with a grin. "Like it needs its own zip code."

"What happens at the park?"

"Just trust us," Trina said.

"The last time you said that, I nearly burned my tongue off with chili infused chocolates."

Lexy grinned. "Yeah, well, you never volunteered to be a taste-tester again, either."

"Lesson learned." He rolled his shoulders and glanced at the bed and the half-packed suitcase. "Okay. I'll come with you."

They left the hotel, and he sat in the third row of an SUV with the park's logo emblazoned on the side. He stared out the window, the conversation between the two couples became background noise as he thought about what might happen when he saw Jenni. Was she angry he hadn't answered her messages? If the situation were reversed, he'd be pissed to be ignored, but he also wouldn't have put anyone ahead of Jenni.

Well, that wasn't entirely true.

If his parents needed him, or Trina or Lexy, he'd have left in a heartbeat to help.

They'd known each other for a day, and he was putting a lot of pressure on things. She'd told him she couldn't spend the night, but when she fell asleep in his arms he didn't wake her up. He'd liked it—liked holding her and watching her sleep. He should have woken her up. Then none of this mess would have happened. Instead, he'd pitched a fit like a little bitch and potentially ruined the most amazing thing that had happened to him in years.

As the SUV pulled down a side road that ran alongside the park, Devlin asked, "Did Jenni ask you to come get me?"

"Nope," Trina said from the second row, turning around to face him as she leaned on the back of the seat. "We offered but she said no. I think she thought you'd come for her today."

"I thought she'd come for me," he admitted.

"Way to be chivalrous," Lexy said from the passenger seat.

"Hey, she walked away from *me*," he pointed out. "I know she called, but she could have come to the hotel to talk to me personally."

"He's got a point," Justus said.

Trina shook her head. "No, he doesn't."

Justus parked the SUV and they got out. Devlin followed them to a large golf cart. Win sat in the driver's seat and Justus, Trina, and Lexy stood next to it.

"What's going on?"

"There are safari tours going on right now," Trina said. "So, to get where you need to go, Win's going to drive you in the golf cart."

"Where do I need to go?"

Lexy kissed Win and then said to Devlin, "Everything will make sense soon, I promise."

He arched his brow at his cousin and then sat down next to Win. He waved as the golf cart took off, heading down a wide path. "We use golf carts to get around the park. Me and my friends work in the garage and handle vehicle maintenance."

"Have you worked here long?"

"I started fixing things when I was a teenager. Did you

know I met Lexy when her tire blew on the way back from a baking competition?"

"Yeah, I heard the story."

"Life's funny like that, I guess." Win said. He lifted a walkie from a holder, twisted the dial on top, and then said, "This is Win. I need a delay on the tours."

There was a crackle and then a masculine voice said, "How long? We've got VIPs waiting."

"Thirty minutes. We have an emergency meeting at the third paddock."

"Um, what?"

"Just don't send anymore tours, and let me know when the lion paddock is clear."

"You bet."

Win hung the walkie back in the holder and put his foot on the gas. The golf cart lurched a little, and then sped up as they maneuvered along the path. Devlin could see that the path ran parallel to another, this one a wide dirt path with tire prints. Beyond the path he could see a fenced in area with elephants. A Jeep left right as they arrived, and they followed them to another paddock with white-tailed deer and buffalo, and then to a paddock full of wolves. They waited while a woman was escorted from the Jeep to the fence by one of two men where she had her picture taken.

"Why is there only one person on the tour at a time?" Devlin asked.

"It's a VIP tour. The Jeep is smaller, so it only holds the driver and the guide, plus the guest and gear. There are larger Jeeps for families to take the tour, but the VIP tours are for individuals."

"Must keep you guys busy with maintaining the Jeeps."

"Oh yeah."

After the woman and her escorts left, they didn't move

until the walkie crackled and a man said, "The lions are clear. You have thirty minutes."

Win answered, "I'll let you know when we're done."

"Where are we going exactly?"

"You'll see."

Win pressed on the gas and they moved along the path. They stopped at the next paddock. "So, go on up there," Win said.

Devlin looked at him in surprise. "Where?"

"The fence."

"Why on earth would I want to do that?"

Win's brow arched. "You told my girl that you trusted her, so you should also trust me."

"I don't know you."

Win grinned broadly and said, "Yeah, well, I'm wonderful." His expression instantly sobered. "Go to the fence."

"And then what?"

"You'll see."

Feeling disgruntled, Devlin got out of the golf cart. He looked at Win, who simply pointed a finger to the paddock. Devlin turned and made his way across the mulch bed that separated the two paths and then walked to the fence. The chain-link fence was tall and topped with barb wire. He curled his fingers around the links and looked inside, where he saw a group of lions. They were all males with big manes, except for one female.

"Lucky girl," he said under his breath.

All the lions looked at him, as if they'd heard him speak. The biggest male made a chuffing sound and then the female raced around the males and headed right for the fence. She was a beautiful lioness, with tawny fur and long whiskers, and when she reached the fence, she rose onto her hind legs and curled her paws around the fence links the same way that he had.

He was six and a half feet tall, and the lioness was just slightly shorter than him standing up. She purred loudly, and rubbed her nose on his fingers. He was so entranced by the sight that it didn't occur to him that he wasn't heeding the posted signs and keeping his fingers off the fence.

"Hey, beautiful," he said as she licked his knuckles. "I have no clue why Win dropped me off here, but I kind of don't mind."

She butted his fingers with her head and stared at him, rising even taller onto her toes until she was looking him square in the eye. She yowled softly and insistently, and he wished he spoke lion. As she yowled again, more earnestly, he was caught by the golden hue of her eyes. They were the same lovely color that he'd sworn he'd seen Jenni's eyes change to when they'd made love. He'd never gotten a chance to ask her about it, because he hadn't really thought he'd witnessed her eyes changing color so dramatically.

"You remind me of Jenni," he said. "Fierce and determined."

She purred loudly and then her eyes changed color from gold to blue. The exact shade of blue as Jenni's.

Devlin took a step back and released the fence. "What the hell?"

The lioness dropped down, pacing in front of the fence. She yowled, more angrily this time, and he distinctly felt like he was being reprimanded. Which was insane on a dozen different levels.

"I think you know why you're here," Win called. "But if you don't, get in the cart and I'll take you somewhere else to figure things out."

He looked at the lioness and she sat on her haunches, her tail curling around her paws. With a last look into her once-more golden eyes, he walked back to the cart and sat down.

"I think I'm going crazy."

"It happens to the best of us," Win said.

"No, I mean really crazy. Like save me a room at the loony bin."

"You're not going crazy," Win said. "It'll make sense soon enough."

The cart stopped in front of a building with a sign that read, "Employee Cafeteria." Trina and Justus stood outside of the building.

"Thanks for the ride," he said to Win as he got out.

"Sure thing. I'll see you."

Devlin walked to the couple and said, "Win said he'd take me somewhere to figure things out."

"Just follow us," Trina said.

Justus entered a code in a security pad next to the door and it unlocked with a loud click. He held the door open for Trina and Devlin followed her inside. There was one large room with round tables and chairs, and a kitchen area with a counter, heat lamps, and several refrigerators.

"I know this seems all weird to you, but I still need you to trust me," Trina said.

"I do. Now that I'm here, though, I'd like to see Jenni."

"We'll take you to her," Justus said.

"Good. I made an ass of myself and I need to apologize."

Trina smiled and held up what looked like a black napkin. "Put this on."

"On what?" he looked at her suspiciously.

"Cover your eyes."

"Why?"

"Oh my gosh! Stop asking questions and just do it."

Trina rolled the napkin and handed it to him, and he gave her a long look and then covered his eyes, tying it behind his head. She put her hand on his elbow and said, "You can't see where we're going."

"I figured that from the blindfold," he said dryly.

"Smartass," she chided, but he could hear the smile in her voice.

They walked slowly and Devlin tried to use his hearing to figure out where they were going, but he was clueless. He did hear Justus enter codes into doors to unlock them, and they went down a set of stairs, but because Devlin was entirely turned around by the time Trina said he could take the blindfold off, he wasn't sure they hadn't left the park.

He blinked at the bright overhead lights, and then he was aware that they weren't alone in the room. Along with Caesar, Jupiter, Trina, and Justus, the lioness was sitting in the center of the room, tail curled around her paws, and her eyes flashing from blue to gold.

An ancient part of him that recognized a predator urged him to run, but there was something really familiar about the lioness, and it wasn't only because he'd seen her in the paddock on the safari tour.

"What's really going on here?" he asked.

Trina slid her hand into his and gave it a squeeze. "It'll be okay."

"What will?" he asked, and then movement caught his attention and he turned to watch the lioness as she stretched, her claws scraping against the floor. She straightened, yowled, and then her whole body began to change shape. The tawny fur receded, replaced by lightly tanned skin. Claws became fingernails, paws became hands and feet. The lioness turned into Jenni, who stood tall, her hands on her hips and her eyes still changing colors.

Devlin wondered briefly if he'd stroked out.

"I, uh," he stumbled over his words, not sure he'd actually seen what he'd seen. "What was that?"

Jenni let out a soft growl. "I just shifted from lion to human."

His mind replayed the scene. He'd seen it. He just wasn't sure he believed it. "Could you do that again?"

Her mouth dropped open. "No! I can't do it again, or I'll be stuck in my shift. I'm kinda ticked at you so you don't really want me to have claws right now."

He stared at the beautiful woman in front of him, and then things slowly started to make sense. He really had witnessed Jenni turn into a lioness. And since he'd never heard of such a thing happening before, then it must be a well-kept secret. Caesar's rules were how she stayed safe.

He looked at his sister, who was smiling up at him, and then he looked at Justus, who had his back turned so he wasn't looking at a very naked Jenni. Which Devlin appreciated.

"How do you know about this?" he asked Trina.

"Justus is a bear shifter and I'm his soulmate."

"Lexy?"

"Win is a gorilla shifter. Caesar and Jupiter are lion shifters, like Jenni."

"The park?"

"It's a cover," Justus said. "Our people live underground in secret, and we run all aspects of the park."

Caesar said, "We have rules for a reason, Devlin. They weren't meant to insult you, but to keep our people safe. We can't just go around telling everyone about what we are, or we potentially endanger all of us."

Suddenly, he wanted to help keep Jenni safe at any cost. And that's when he knew why she'd never be able to move to Rhode Island. She was safest in the park with her people.

"Can you give us the room?" he asked.

Trina kissed his cheek and he whispered a word of thanks to her. When the room was empty, he faced Jenni, ready to lay his cards on the table.

CHAPTER SEVEN

Jenni had been hanging out at the paddock for the VIP tours, hoping that one of the lions would find his soulmate among the patrons.

"Psst!" a feminine voice said.

Jenni's ears twitched and she looked around and saw Trina in the storage building's open doorway. She motioned for Jenni to join her, and she padded over to her. Caesar followed, his whiskers bristling in curiosity.

"Hey," Trina said. "We brought my brother here. Win is taking him on the tour in a golf cart, and he's going to stop here at the paddock so that Dev can see you in your form. Then we thought you could meet us down in the meeting hall so that you can shift for him."

Jenni's eyes widened. She wished she could speak, because she had a million things to say, chief among them was how Trina had managed to get Devlin to the park when the asshole hadn't answered any of her calls or texts.

As if knowing what she was asking, Trina smiled. "Lex and I went with our mates and brought him here. Sometimes guys need a helping hand to get to the right place. Or a friendly shove."

Jenni purred and nodded, excitement coursing through her. It had taken about a half hour, but she'd heard the golf cart as it pulled up and idled on the maintenance path in front of the paddock. Devlin had been confused, but he'd still approached the fence, and she'd raced right to him. She'd even let her humanity show through her eyes so he could see the change.

Once she'd shifted in front of him, she'd felt entirely exposed and it wasn't just because she was naked. If Devlin freaked out because of her shifting, he'd still be stuck in the park. The council would never let him leave now that he knew the secret. In a way, she was thankful that Trina and Lexy had intervened because it forced him to see why she couldn't leave the park.

She twisted her fingers together and inhaled deeply, trying to calm her flying pulse. She opened her mouth, but he put his hand up.

"Before you say anything, I was mad last night because you picked your friends over me. I know it was childish not to answer your calls, but I just didn't want to face a decision of my own."

She tilted her head. "What decision?"

"Resigning from my job and moving to New Jersey."

Her breath caught in her throat. "Are you... what are you saying?"

He closed the distance between them and put his hands on her waist. "I didn't understand why you had to leave last night, and I was too pissed to think that there was anything other than you not wanting to be with me at the heart of it."

"I wanted to stay, I really did."

"I had a chance to wake you up and send you on your way, but I didn't want to. I was selfish, and I thought you were just being cautious because we hadn't known each other long. I'm sorry for that."

"I'm sorry I couldn't tell you why. Unmated males and females aren't allowed to stay outside of the park overnight."

"I should have been more understanding. So, the shifting thing? It's fucking cool as hell."

She grinned. "I'm glad you think so."

He sobered immediately, his gaze hardening. "Your safety is paramount to me now. I would never jeopardize the secret that keeps you and your people safe." He took a single step back and took her hands in his. "Ask me what you need to ask me."

She blinked in surprise, and then smiled as warm tingles skirted up and down her spine. "Devlin, will you be my mate?"

"It's special, right? It's why I can't get you out of my head even though I'm human?"

She nodded. "We're soulmates. My people believe that there's one person for each shifter, that us and our beasts will recognize on sight. You're that male for me."

"And you're the woman for me. Yes, I'll be your mate, Jenni."

He pulled her close, enveloping her in a tight hug. He kissed her, his tongue dipping into her mouth for only a heartbeat before he cleared his throat and said, "For obvious reasons you can't leave the park. I want to be with you. I wanted to be with you from the moment I saw you. The intensity scared me, but it makes sense now. It's supposed to be hard and fast like that because it's different for your kind to be together than if I was with a human."

"You're amazing," she said.

"Well, I did act like an ass for a while, and I'm sorry if I made you feel bad. I was hurt."

She rested her head over his heart. "I'm sorry."

"Don't be. You need to be safe. And our kids—can we have kids?"

Her head shot up and she saw his face twisted with worry. "Kids already? We just met."

He grinned. "I like to move fast, sweetheart."

"Yes, we can have kids. They'll most likely be able to shift."

"Awesome. I don't suppose you could bite me and turn me, like in the TV shows?"

She made a face. "What shows are you watching? No, I can't. Weres are born, not made."

"Now, I'm going to point out that you're naked and you smell incredible."

"How do I smell?"

"Like sunshine and dry grass, but also sweet. Of course, I know exactly how you taste and I can't wait to taste you again."

"We can go to my place," she said. "Each group has a private living area, and me and the pride members each have our own house."

"How many pride members?"

"Eight including me."

He stopped her before she could open the door. "Um, you're naked."

"Nudity isn't a big deal."

"It is to me, because you just said that you're mine and I'm yours, and I don't want anyone seeing what's *mine*."

He pulled off his t-shirt and handed it to her. She tugged it on, loving how it was still warm and smelled like him, all heat and male.

"There," he said, giving her a peck on the lips. "Much better."

He held the door open for her and then took her hand,

and she led him out of the meeting room and through the marketplace.

"Two of the mates have a nail salon here," she said. "Jupiter's mate, Celeste, and Zane's mate, Adriana. They both did that aboveground before they became mates."

"Does everyone work at the park in one way or another?"

"Pretty much. It's not encouraged for our people to work outside of the park. There's safety within these walls."

"That makes sense."

"The marketplace is where we can get meals and place orders for any items we need. There is a shop stocked with basic necessities, and of course we're not actually trapped in the park and can go out shopping or to eat whenever we want."

"That's good. I'd like to take you on a real date."

"I'd like that, too."

They reached the lions' private living area, and she entered the code. "I'll share the codes with you. We have one for our area and for the entrances to go topside. We can get up to the park through the employee cafeteria and the storage building in the paddock."

He followed her inside.

"Our private area is decorated to resemble the Savannah, it makes our lions feel at home."

He turned in a slow circle and whistled. "This is pretty damn impressive."

They walked to the row of homes, and she opened the door to hers. "This is home sweet home."

"Are the homes all the same?"

"Pretty much. Some have more or less bedrooms. Mine has three bedrooms."

The family room had a denim-blue couch with blue and white striped throw pillows. A flat-screen TV sat on a glass stand, with her collection of Blu-Ray romantic comedies lined up next to the player on one of the shelves.

He didn't say anything as he looked around the room.

"Are you okay?"

He met her gaze. "Yeah. I was just wondering about my job."

She felt bad that he was going to lose the promotion he'd been working so hard for, but there was no way that she could move to Rhode Island with him. They could try the long-distance thing, but her beast was not interested in spending any time away from their mate.

"I'm sorry."

He shook his head. "Don't be. I just want to be able to support you and take care of you. I'll find a good job somewhere else. The important thing is that at the end of the day, you and I are together."

"I agree."

"Want to see the bedroom?" she asked with a purr.

"Hell yes."

There was a knock at the door, and she sighed. "Hold that thought."

She opened the door and smiled at Caesar.

"Sorry for the interruption, but I wanted to talk to you two about the mating ceremony," Caesar said.

"What's a mating ceremony?" Devlin asked.

Caesar had a leather-bound notebook in his hand. "Have a seat," he said, gesturing to the couch. He disappeared into the kitchen and returned with a kitchen chair, which he placed across the coffee table from them and sat down. "Lions have certain customs when it comes to mating. It's not enough to just say 'let's be mates' and have sex, we honor our ancestors and pride by performing certain rituals."

"Like getting married?"

Jenni said, "We can get married if you'd like, but that's a human custom."

"You don't want to get married?"

"I do. But the mating ceremony is different."

Caesar nodded. "A marriage could be ended, but a mating is permanent. Once you enter into it with Jenni, there isn't anything that will break it. You could walk away, but her lion wouldn't allow her to be with anyone else. It's why understanding mating is so important, since your people don't have the same sort of primal instincts that ours do."

"I'm not going anywhere."

Jenni nudged him with her shoulder. "I know that. Just think of our mating ceremonies as traditions. It's important to me and my lion."

"Then it's important to me, too."

His words warmed her all over. She wanted to rub against him and purr, but with her alpha right there, she opted to just smile. She'd rub on him *later*.

"Our traditions are built on the assumption that the male is a shifter," Caesar said, clearing his throat, "which is why I wanted to come speak to you. I spoke to Jupiter about changing some aspects of the tradition, but depending on what we need to prepare, I didn't want to wait until tomorrow to talk to you both. Normally, we'd handle the mating traditions on your first night together here, but things are different with you two, so we'll plan for tomorrow night."

She listened as Caesar explained the first tradition, where the male proved his worth to his mate and pride by hunting and killing an animal at night. When Jupiter mated Celeste, he'd hunted a rabbit in the lion paddock after the park was closed, killed and dressed it, and then cooked it over a fire and fed it to her. Jenni knew that although Devlin was strong, he wasn't a trained hunter and even a well-trained human would have a hard time catching a rabbit in the dark.

"Instead of foregoing the hunting tradition entirely, I'm suggesting that the two of you work together."

Her brows rose. "What do you mean?"

"I mean that we release a rabbit, you shift, and the two of you hunt, kill, and clean it together. It's not quite the same, but it allows you to participate in that part of our traditions. You'll prove to each other that you can work together to provide for your family, which is what the tradition is about."

"Cool," Devlin said. "I'll get to see you in your shift again, and hunt with you."

Jenni's eyes stung with tears. She hadn't thought she'd get to share that tradition with Devlin, but her alpha had changed things for them.

"Tomorrow, you'll come to my home at noon for lunch with the pride. It will give everyone a chance to meet and get to know you. Then you'll harvest and prepare the prickly pears and make the lily bands. We'll have the mating ceremony tomorrow night, and then you'll hunt. The pride will leave you alone in the paddock to complete your mating. Devlin will officially become a member of the pride."

"I need to go home at some point," Devlin said. "I have to resign my job in person on Monday and pack up my home. Not to mention that I need to talk to my parents and tell them the good news."

"I have Monday and Tuesday off work," Jenni said.

Caesar nodded. "I'd recommend taking either some pride members to help you pack up, or your sister and cousin, and their mates."

Devlin nodded. "Thanks, Caesar."

"You're welcome. See you for lunch tomorrow."

He shook Devlin's hand and left, and then turned to Jenni with a growl that was adorably human. "Bedroom. Now."

"Tour?" she asked attempting to play innocent.

"Eventually," he said, stalking to her, his muscles bunching as he moved gracefully, looking every inch the predator. Her lioness preened in happiness. He wasn't a lion, but he was fierce.

He bent and put his shoulder into her abdomen and hauled her over his shoulder. She laughed as she found herself upside down, his cute butt right in front of her. Giving him a pinch on the cheek she said, "I love how your mind works, I think you're psychic."

"If you were thinking about getting naked and playing a game of how many orgasms I can give you, then yes, I *am* psychic."

She shivered at the sexy threat, a purr rumbling in her chest. It was going to be a magnificent night.

CHAPTER EIGHT

The next morning, Devlin followed Jenni to the greenhouse that was in the lions' private area. She opened the door and the scents of earth and flowers filled the air around them. She grabbed two baskets and tools and handed him one of the baskets and a pair of shears.

"First, we'll harvest the prickly pear, and I'll show you how to clean it in the house."

"I've never had that before," he said.

"It's part of our ceremony. It's delicious, but it's a hassle to clean."

She cut the pears from the plant and put them in his basket. Then she led the way to a table that held rows of lilies.

"These are Impala Lilies, which are native to Africa. We plant them in cycles so that at any given time, there are enough blooming for a mating ceremony. Before our people used greenhouses, the flowers would be cut and dried and saved for later use. It's much nicer to use fresh flowers, though.

"The number of stems relates to the members of our immediate family. I'm counting my pride as my immediate family instead of my biological family. You have both parents and your sister and her mate, which means we need eleven stems for each bracelet, and we'll make two of them for me to wear."

She began to cut the stems and urged him to do the same. He set the basket of prickly pears down and used the shears on the plants, snipping off the pretty flowers until they'd collected twenty-two, laying them gently in her basket. They put the tools back on their hooks and returned to her house, where she showed him how to safely peel the thick outer skin of the prickly pear and prepare it for that night.

"I wanted to talk to you about the marking."

"Marking what?" he asked.

She flashed him a grin. "Me marking you. With my fangs."

He stopped, knife poised above the fruit. "You want to put your fangs in me?"

"Yes. Me and my lion do. Tonight, after we hunt and have the ceremony with my pride, they'll leave us alone in the paddock so we can solidify our mating. After we make love, my fangs will elongate and I'll bite your neck."

"Sounds painful."

"I promise that I'll be gentle, and hopefully you'll be really blissed out on the after-sex glow and won't feel it as much."

"I like that idea."

She exhaled like she'd been holding her breath. "Good. I have fast healing, so you can bite me but it won't scar like my fangs will in your flesh. I hope you don't feel bad about that."

He hummed, turning his attention back to the fruit. "Will your lioness be upset?"

"No, of course not. You're my soulmate. That you aren't a shifter doesn't matter to me."

"Good. I just don't want you to feel like you're missing out on anything because I'm human."

"I don't, I promise. I'm so happy to be with you. All the other stuff is just unimportant details."

"I'm happy to be with you, too."

When the cut fruit was cooling in the refrigerator in a bowl, they sat on the couch and she showed him how to braid the flower stems into a bracelet. By the time they were finished making the two bracelets, the sweet scent of the flowers was all over them, and he thought he'd never be able to smell the flowers again without thinking about how beautiful she was and how deftly her fingers worked the flower stems.

"Ready for lunch?" she asked.

"Truthfully? I'd rather take you to bed."

She purred. "I'd love that, too, but there's time for that tonight. If we don't go to Caesar's, he's going to come here, so we might as well just go."

He chuckled. She put the bracelets in the refrigerator, covered with damp paper towels to keep them from wilting, and then they walked to Caesar's home. The pride was gathered in the kitchen at an enormous table.

"Have a seat," Caesar said.

The table was set with platters and trays of food, from grilled meats to roasted vegetables. He sat next to Jenni, with Caesar on his right at the head of the table. The dishes were passed around, and he and Jenni filled their plates. While they ate, the pride asked him questions about his life in Rhode Island and shared the history of the pride with him.

"What are you going to tell your parents?" Amadeus asked.

"I don't have a clue. Trina told them that her job at the shop came with an apartment, and so did Lexy. I don't think

I can say I have one of the apartments in the park if I'm not actually working here, and it also would look really weird I think."

"How would it be weird?" Caesar asked.

"Well, truthfully it's kind of odd to have room and board with jobs nowadays. I haven't heard of anything like that outside of the big theme parks, and they don't have apartments in a converted barn, they have dormitories."

Xavier said, "We hadn't thought about that. It does seem kind of odd."

Caesar said, "It's important for the mates to live at the park, so we created the apartment building so that if any parents or family members came to visit, they would be able to show them an actual place."

Jenni had explained that there was only one real apartment in the barn. The other two were simply facades. He thought it was damn lucky that his and Trina's parents, and Lexy's parents, hadn't wanted to see their apartments at the same time, or they would have been in trouble.

"We need to address this with the council," Lucius said. "The more soulmates that are found, the more we'll have a need for a cover story. It could get messy really quickly."

"How are you finding your soulmates now?" Devlin asked.

"Our people rely on our beasts to help lead us to our soulmate," Caesar said, leaning back in his chair. "For many years, none of our people were finding our soulmates, so several months ago the council decided to create a VIP tour for single males and females in the tri-state area."

"Oh," Devlin said. "I wondered why there was only one person in the Jeep last night. Win said they were special tours, but I'd never heard of such a thing. Now I get it. By having the individual tours, if one of the patrons happens to be a soulmate, the shifter would know and you'd be able to deal with it."

Jenni nodded. "So far, only two mates have come from the tours—Celeste and Adriana."

Celeste smiled from across the table. "They thought more mates would come from the tours, but so far not so much."

"How many tours are there a day?"

"We run them Friday, Saturday, and Sunday from four to eight p.m.," Xavier said. "We take turns with tours and handling security for the park. We can't *all* be in the paddock all the time, or something could go wrong and no one would be there to handle it."

"You can meet your mate in person, though, right? You don't have to be in your shift."

"We recognize our soulmate in any form. Like how you and Jenni were immediately drawn to each other," Jupiter said.

"Even though I'm human," Celeste said, "I was smitten with Jupiter from the moment I saw him. It was weird to feel connected to a lion, and of course he tried to take the fence down with his claws when he saw me."

Everyone at the table laughed.

"I'm going to talk to the council at our next meeting about the housing situation," Caesar. "I don't think it's enough anymore to have the barn."

"Have you thought about building an actual dormitory on the property?" Devlin asked.

Caesar's brows rose. "No."

"The more mates that come here, the more chance for family to come along and want to know more, too. It would be easy enough to build a simple dormitory structure, somewhere on the park's property but not accessible by any patrons. I was actually thinking about buying a house somewhere near here, and just using it as an address and a place for my family to come visit."

"We could buy a development outside of the zoo," Jupiter said. "That way if any mates have jobs outside of the zoo, they don't have to explain why they are living *in* the zoo."

"No, it needs to be on our property, the council would never go for something off-site. But," Caesar said, rubbing his chin in thought, "the park owns the properties on either side and behind the park. The properties were bought so that no one could build anywhere near us, and if we ever needed to expand, we could. The land is there to use."

"It would be a shame to lose all that hard work we put into the fake apartments," Mercer said, "but it seems like being prepared in advance is better than having to rush."

"It sounds like a great idea," Jenni said. "Plus, if anyone finds their soulmate, they'd have a place to go to take their soulmate for privacy if they needed it."

"It's not *if*, it's *when* we find our soulmates," Javan said with a grin.

Jenni nodded. "Right. *When*."

"I'll convene the council to discuss this idea, but I think it has merit." Caesar lifted his glass and said, "A toast to Jenni and Devlin. May we all find our soulmates."

The lions lifted their glasses in cheer, and Jenni kissed Devlin and smiled. "I'm so happy you came to see your cousin's shop."

"Me too, sweetheart."

~

Devlin looked at the black leather pants that Jupiter had brought for him to wear for the mating ceremony. He tugged them up his legs and fastened them, then he sat on the bed and reached for his shoes.

"No shoes," Jenni said, coming out of the bathroom. She was wearing a long, black t-shirt that barely covered her cute butt.

"Tell me again why we have to wear black and no shoes?"

"First of all, it's tradition, and secondly, it keeps us from drawing unnecessary attention to ourselves while we're in the paddock. We *are* going to have a bonfire, but the black clothing helps to obscure us."

They stopped in the kitchen and she carried the flowers and he carried the bowl of cut prickly pears, and they left her house and headed to the far side of the pride's private area. There was a security door, which he hadn't noticed when he'd checked the area out before.

"This leads directly up into the storage building in our paddock. Each group has their own paddock entrance, too."

They climbed a set of stairs and then she entered a code into another security pad, which unlocked the door in the ceiling. She gave the door a push and it opened fully, and he couldn't see anything beyond the door except darkness. She led him into the shed and turned on a soft, low light. After she closed and secured the door in the floor, she said, "I just wanted to say thank you."

"For what, sweetheart?"

"I know this is all new and probably very strange to you, and I'm glad that you're not resistant to the traditions of my people. It means the world to me that you're willing to do all this for me."

"I'm crazy about you. I would absolutely do anything to make you happy."

She purred softly and even though he couldn't see her well, he could tell she was smiling. "I'm happy now that you're in my life."

She moved to the shed's door and opened it, stepping outside. He followed, watching as she extinguished the light and then shut the door. He handed her the bowl of fruit and lifted her into his arms. Even though she'd said she could walk, Jupiter had mentioned that he'd carried Celeste, and Devlin wanted to do that, too. Plus, he'd take any opportunity to hold her. In the distance, he could see the faint glow of a fire, and he followed it. It was tempting to look down and try to see where he was going, but he wouldn't be able to see anything anyway, and Jenni promised that there were no holes or objects laying around in the paddock.

When he reached the fire, there were eight figures around a bonfire, with a dark colored fur rug on the ground next to it. Devlin set Jenni on her feet and smiled at the group. Everyone was wearing black, including Celeste, who stood in Jupiter's arms.

"Alpha Caesar," Jenni said, "I present my soulmate, Devlin, to you."

Caesar joined them. "Welcome, Devlin. As alpha, it's my honor to welcome you to our pride. Do you come tonight of your own free will, to accept Jenni as your mate?"

"Yes," Devlin said.

The pride growled in approval.

"Prepare for the hunt," Caesar said.

Jenni stepped a few paces from the bonfire and Devlin joined her, watching as she pulled off the t-shirt. Jenni shifted, and Devlin watched in fascination as she turned from beautiful woman to stunning lioness. He stroked the soft fur on the top of her head, rubbing her ears lightly, and smiling as she tilted her head in encouragement.

They joined the pride once more, and Caesar handed Devlin a hunting knife in a sheath, which he secured to his waistband.

"Prove yourselves worthy of each other," Caesar said. "Good luck."

Xavier appeared with a small cage holding a brown

rabbit. He opened the cage and lifted the rabbit out, setting it on the ground. In a heartbeat, the rabbit took off into the darkness. Jenni growled and followed after it with Devlin on her tail. With the starlight and moon providing some illumination, he was able to see Jenni's shadowy form as she chased the rabbit, and he stayed as close as he could. Jenni snarled, jumping to the side, and he saw her hit the ground and roll, her claws digging into the earth. He saw the rabbit head his way, and he lunged for it, grabbing a leg as it darted away from him. He landed on his knees, not letting go of the rabbit, which squealed in desperation. Jenni growled and joined him, and he held the wiggling creature up to her. She snagged it in her jaws and bit down, ending its life swiftly.

Devlin smelled blood as she opened her mouth and he took the rabbit from her. "That was cool as hell," he whispered, stroking her head. He'd expected to just watch her stalk and kill the rabbit, but he'd actually been able to help out.

He carried the rabbit back to the bonfire, unable to stop the grin. It was exhilarating. Jenni shifted back into her human form and put on the black t-shirt, joining him next to the fire. He'd never butchered an animal before, so he gave it to her and watched as she efficiently skinned and cleaned it, threading the carcass onto a long piece of metal, which she laid over two other pieces that were imbedded in the ground on either side of the bonfire. She attached a turning handle, and he added more wood to the fire at her direction.

"It takes about forty-five minutes to cook," Jenni said.

"In the meantime," Caesar said, "We'll do the other part of our ceremony."

Jenni took his hand and led him to the fur rug. They knelt on it and faced each other. Caesar picked up the bracelets from where Jenni had set them down.

"Impala Lilies come from Africa, the place of our shifter

ancestors. It's important that we hold tight to the traditions of our people so that we never forget what we are or where we came from. The fierce beasts that prowled in the darkest nights cherished their mates above all else. It's because of these fierce protective instincts that our beasts must mark our mates, a visible claim that not only permanently imprints the mate's scent on the skin, but also scars it.

"Devlin, do you accept your place at Jenni's side as her beloved mate? Do you swear to protect her to the best of your abilities, as well as any young that you might have? Do you welcome the marking from her beast tonight, knowing in your heart that this is truly the first night of the rest of your mated life?"

"I accept Jenni, her beast, and her marks."

Caesar placed the bracelets on Jenni's wrists and she pushed them up past her elbows.

Devlin lifted the bowl of prickly pears and held it in his hands.

"Jenni," Caesar said, "do you swear yourself and your lioness to Devlin? Do you promise to make his life as sweet as the prickly pear, as lovely as the lilies, and to protect him with claw and fang as long as you live?"

"I swear," Jenni said.

She picked up a piece of fruit and fed it to Devlin, and then he fed her a piece. They took turns, until the bowl was empty. He set it on the ground away from the fire. Caesar placed his hands on top of their heads and smiled down at them.

"I welcome you, Devlin, to the pride, and declare this night that when Jenni has marked and mated you, you will be as a lion in the pride, honored and accepted. The pride will stand with you. May your cubs be as strong and fierce as their parents."

The lions roared in approval, Jenni lifting her head and

joining in. Devlin loved the sound, one of welcome and approval. When the rabbit was finished cooking, he and Jenni shared the meat with each other, and also the pride. Then each pride member dropped a lily on the rug as a token of their approval and a blessing on the mating. They disappeared quickly into the darkness.

"I think we're alone now," he said.

"Hold on," Jenni said, tilting her head and listening. In the distance, he heard a very faint clang. Then she smiled. *"Now, we're alone."*

He cupped her face and kissed her. "I'm so ready for tonight."

"Me, too. You're wonderful, and I'm honored and lucky to have a soulmate as amazing as you."

"I'm the one who's lucky and honored, Jenni. You're more than I ever hoped for or knew I even needed. I'd be lost without you."

"Neither of us will be lost, again."

They stripped each other quickly and made love, their bodies joining together again and again. When he was entirely, blissfully worn out, he offered her his neck. She purred, flashing her sharp fangs a moment before she pressed them into his flesh. He'd expected it would hurt, like being stabbed by two needles, but all he felt was pressure and then a sweet connection that bloomed between him and his mate.

He'd never known that soulmates were real. He'd always suspected they were born more of fantasy and dreams than reality. But he believed in them now, because he was holding his soulmate in his arms, feeling her soft skin and her warm heat, and the thick fangs in his neck. She lifted from him, lapping at his wound with a stuttering purr. He turned his head and bit her, knowing that it was only symbolic because he didn't have real fangs. She writhed in his arms with a happy sigh.

"I'm utterly yours," he whispered against her skin before kissing the mark he'd made. "One hundred percent."

"Me, too. I can't wait to see what our future holds."

"A lot of love," he promised. "And a lot of happiness."

CHAPTER NINE

Jenni grabbed the bath towels from the cabinet under the sink in Devlin's apartment and stuffed them into a trash bag. Her mate was in the bedroom, packing his clothes and she'd volunteered to handle the bathroom. They'd left early Monday morning for Rhode Island. She'd never been that far north, and enjoyed the scenery and getting to know him and his family better.

He'd dropped her off at his apartment and then gone to his office to quit his job. She'd worried that he would grow to resent her after having to give up something he'd been looking forward to, but he said he'd rather have her and find a new job, than be without her for even a minute. When he'd returned two hours later, he'd been quiet for a while, eventually explaining that his bosses had been disappointed that he was quitting so abruptly and not even giving them notice so they could find a replacement. They'd offered him a salary increase and some other perks, but he'd politely refused. He was worried about finding a decent job without his company's recommendation, but she promised that it would all work out.

"How can you be sure?" he asked.

She shrugged. "I don't know. Because I feel like now that we're together, the rest will come with time."

"You're very optimistic."

"You make it sound like a bad thing."

"It's not, sweetheart, but I just want to be able to take care of you. Having a good job is the foundation of that. I think you don't understand because you didn't have to interview for your job—you live in the zoo, and you work there. But for me, I have to go into employers and try to explain why I walked away from a great job without notice."

He'd kissed her and headed into the bedroom to pack, and she'd been left feeling like she was the source of some serious issues. She didn't want their mating to be effected by his job issues, but her lioness absolutely didn't care about anything that would take him from her. All the shifters in the park worked there, and the mates did, too. Devlin was a big guy, but he wasn't interested in being a security guard, and he couldn't fix cars to work with the gorillas, cook with the bears, take care of animals with the elephants, or run the tours with the wolves.

Justus, Trina, and Lexy had come along to help pack, and had overheard their conversation.

"It's part of being a human guy," Trina said. "His self-worth as a mate is wrapped up in his ability to provide for you."

Justus said, "But the park provides everything."

"It's not the same," Lexy said. "And he worked hard to get where he was with his career."

Trina smiled gently. "I'm sure it will work out. He probably feels guilty for quitting without notice, and of course he's lying to our parents about some things and that's difficult, too. I have trouble with it myself."

Jenni hated the lies, too, but the safety of the park residents demanded a total blackout of information to anyone who was not a shifter or a mate.

Devlin appeared from the bedroom, dropped two packing boxes, and pulled her gently away from the group. "Hey," he said, cupping her face. "I don't regret a damn thing, okay? I'm concerned about my ability to take care of you, but that's on me and not you. I don't want you to feel guilty about anything. We're together and that's the most important thing to me."

She smiled up at him, her heart tugging at the determined tone of his voice. "Okay."

"Let's get packed up so we can have dinner with my parents and then go home."

"I wish we could stay here tonight," she said. "I'd like to be in your world for a little while."

"There isn't anything in this world for me anymore but my family. Your world is mine now, and I'm ready to go home."

They returned to their packing, and she finished up the bathroom and then pushed a box out into the hall, dragging the bag of towels behind her.

"Bathroom's done," she said.

He straightened and haphazardly folded the sheets that he'd just stripped from the bed. "Good. When we're ready to tell my parents about the move, I'll ask them to sell whatever furniture we leave behind."

For now, he wasn't telling his parents that he'd quit his job and was moving to New Jersey, and he wasn't canceling the lease for his apartment. Once he found a job, then he'd give notice for the apartment and tell his parents. All they knew at the moment was that he and Jenni were *dating*, which, according to Trina, was the first human step before marriage. Humans would think it odd for a man to just quit his job and move after knowing a woman only a few days.

For shifters, though, it made perfect sense. Once a shifter found his or her mate, the need to be with them overwhelmed everything else.

"I want to take my recliner," he said. "It's really comfy."

"I know just the place for it. And it matches my couch, too."

"Kitchen's done," Lexy said, coming into the bedroom. "I'm freaking starving. My folks are coming to your parents' house for dinner, and we need to leave in about ten minutes. How are things coming?"

"Great," Devlin said. "I'm just about done in here."

They hurried to finish packing up his things, and carried them out to the trailer that they'd pulled behind one of the park's SUVs. They left the trailer in the apartment parking lot and drove to Devlin and Trina's parents' home.

Lexy chuckled. "Win just texted and said he wishes everyone luck meeting our crazy family."

Win had needed to work and hadn't been able to take a day off to join them for the trip. Jenni had met Trina and Devlin's parents at the shop, but things were different now that they were together.

"It's crazy, isn't it?" Trina asked.

"What?" Devlin asked.

"That just a couple weeks ago we were all unmated and wondering what the future would hold for us. Now, we're all mated and living at the zoo, and shifters—which seemed like an impossibility—are real."

Devlin glanced at Jenni and took her hand. "If I never said it before, Lex, I'm thankful for your flat tire, because it kicked off the chain of events that brought me and my Jenni together."

"You're welcome," Lexy said with a laugh. "I *am* glad that my bad luck led to something amazing for all of us."

When they arrived at the house, Devlin introduced her to

his parents as his girlfriend. He'd already told them on the phone that he and Jenni were dating, but this was the first time she was meeting them in what she felt was an official capacity. She wanted his parents to like her and think she was a good mate for him to have, even though her lioness didn't particularly care if they liked her or not.

"It's nice to see you again," Betty, Devlin's mom said, giving Jenni a hug. "I *knew* I saw sparks between you two."

"It would have been hard to miss those sparks," Rick, Devlin's dad, said as he kissed her cheek. "How was the drive?"

"Good," Jenni said. "I'm glad to be here, thanks for inviting me."

Rick shut the front door and said, "You're welcome."

Betty ushered them into the living room where Jenni was introduced to Lexy's parents. They all sat and talked for a while before dinner. Devlin's parents asked Jenni about working in the shop with Lexy and Trina. They didn't ask about her family, but she had a feeling they were being polite, since she knew that Devlin had told them about her mom leaving when she was younger and her dad being absent her whole life. She didn't want them to feel sorry for her, because she'd had a great life in the park with Caesar and the pride. What she'd been missing as a kid had been given back to her in spades.

Over a dinner of grilled tilapia topped with thinly sliced mango and sautéed carrots, Jenni heard how Betty and Rick met, laughed at the funny stories of Devlin's childhood, and had a slice of amazing apple pie that Lexy had brought. By the time the evening was over, she hadn't wanted to say goodbye to his parents because she liked them so much. It was easy to see why Devlin and Trina were such amazing people—because their parents were, too.

"Thank you for everything, I had a great time," Jenni said as she hugged Betty.

"I'm so glad. Come back to visit anytime."

"And thanks for the taffy," Rick said. "I'm going to hoard it and eat it all myself."

"No, you won't," Betty warned.

"You'll see," Rick said with a wink. "I'll hide it."

Lexy told Jenni that bringing gifts to parents at the first meeting was a good idea, so she'd brought a bag of different flavors of taffy.

"I'll bring two bags next time," Jenni said.

"I'll find two hiding spots, then," Rick said.

"Watch me hide your favorite coffee mug," Betty said.

"Oh, ouch. Fine, I'll share."

Jenni smiled at their bantering and said goodbye, walking out with Devlin.

He put his arm around Jenni. "They like you, but I knew they would."

She grinned. "I like them, too."

After Lexy, Trina, and Justus joined them, they headed back to Devlin's apartment and hooked up the trailer. As they started the journey back to the park, Jenni leaned on Devlin's shoulder and yawned.

He kissed the top of her head. "It's been a good day."

"Long, but good."

"I'm ready to go home now, though."

"Me, too."

∼

Wednesday morning, Devlin walked Jenni to the sweets shop. They'd unpacked his things the day before, and when she'd gotten dressed for work, she'd loved to see his clothes hanging next to hers in the closet. They'd only been together for a little while, but she already couldn't imagine her life without him. Which was how things were supposed to be with soulmates.

"Hey!" Caesar called to them as they passed by the security office. "Come in here for a minute."

They turned and headed for the office, and found Caesar and the other alphas standing at the counter in the main room.

"Good morning," Jenni said, and then introduced Devlin to the alphas. "Devlin, this is Joss the wolf alpha, Alastair, the elephant alpha, Marcus, the bear alpha, and Atticus, the gorilla alpha. This is my soulmate, Devlin Potter."

Devlin shook the alphas' hands and said, "It's nice to meet you."

"We've been discussing a few things since you two mated," Caesar said. "We understand that you're a finance professional."

"I am. I was up for the controller position at the accounting firm I worked at, and I just recently graduated with my Masters in Finance."

"We'd like to offer you a job at the park," Caesar said.

Jenni's brows rose and her heart sped up with excitement.

Joss said, "We'd like to ask you to join our finance department. Several of my wolves handle things, but we outsource a good deal to a local accounting firm. It would be nice to be able to bring that in-house, especially with someone of your expertise."

"That would be great," Devlin said.

"We've got calls in to several contractors to get bids for the apartment complex that we're going to build for future mates," Atticus said. "But in the meanwhile, we'd like you to find a house or apartment to rent in one of the nearby communities. The park will pay the rent for as long as you need it."

Jenni asked, "Why can't he say he lives in the barn apartments? There are three of them."

Devlin shook his head. "What if my parents came to visit and they wanted to see mine and Trina's apartment? Only one apartment is finished."

"Oh," she said. "Good point. But the same could go for Lexy and Trina."

"Fortunately," Atticus said, "both sets of parents haven't wanted to see the apartments together, but it was a worry. For now, we're going to finish one of the other barn apartments to alleviate that situation, and then eventually there will be a complex that will have a separate entrance instead of being inside the park."

"Cool," Jenni said.

Caesar smiled at her. "After you take Jenni to the shop, come back here and Joss will take you to the finance office so you can meet the wolves. You can take a day or two and think about the job, and then let us know."

Devlin shook the hands of all the alphas again and thanked them for the opportunity. He held the door open for Jenni and then followed her out of the building. She hugged him tightly with a laugh as the door shut.

He laughed and lifted her off the ground. "That's freaking amazing."

"It sure is," she said, kissing him.

"Did you know they were going to do that?" he asked as he set her on the ground and held her hand while they walked toward the shop.

"No. It was in the back of my mind that, so far, they've found jobs for the mates in the park, but in both those instances, the mates created those new jobs. Adriana and Celeste have the nail salon in the market, and Lexy and Trina have the sweets shop. I don't know anything about the finance stuff, so I didn't know if there was room for another person or if I should even ask."

"Well, I was pretty determined to find something on my own," he said. "But this is more than I could have hoped for. Now I don't have to leave the park to go to work, and we can have lunch together."

She stopped and he turned to face her.

"I was afraid you'd resent me for all that you had to give up in order to be with me."

"Never, sweetheart. Before I met you, my career was the most important thing to me. I was confused by my feelings for you at first, and yes, I was reluctant to walk away from my job, but that's because I didn't understand your needs. Now, I know that the place I was always meant to be was here at Amazing Adventures. I not only get *you*, but I also get a job without having to interview for months and then explain why I want to take off Mondays and Tuesdays."

He wiggled his brows at her and she laughed.

"You make me and my lioness so happy. I want only the best for you, and I want you to be as happy as you make me."

"I'm happier now than I've ever been because of you. What I thought of as being happy before, I now see wasn't anything close to real happiness. You're gorgeous and sweet, and most importantly, you're mine."

He made a soft growling sound in his throat, the human equivalent of a happy lion, and he brushed his lips against hers. She deepened the kiss immediately, putting her arms around his neck and pulling him close. Passion flared between them, and if it hadn't been for the tinkling of the bell over the sweets shop door as one of her co-workers opened it, she would have happily forgotten about work entirely.

"Just making sure that you didn't get lost," Trina said.

Devlin groaned in annoyance. "Uncool, Trin."

"That's what sisters are for."

Jenni smiled up at Devlin. "Come back for lunch?"

"You bet," he said.

"Have fun with the wolves," she said, giving his hand a little squeeze. "Oh, I almost forgot."

"What, sweetheart?"

"You're sexy as hell, you make me feel like the most important female in the world, and you're *mine*, too."

He grinned. "See you soon, soulmate."

She didn't want to part, but she couldn't help but enjoy the view as he walked away, his sexy butt covered in tight denim that made her want to pounce on him. Her cat purred in happiness.

"Let's get to work so we can get to lunch," Jenni said as she walked into the shop.

"Lunch is my favorite time of the workday," Lexy said.

"My favorite is when we're done working," Trina said.

"I think going home with Devlin will be my favorite thing about the day," Jenni said. "And waking up with him, too."

"There's nothing better than being in your soulmate's arms," Lexy said.

Jenni agreed wholeheartedly.

CHAPTER TEN

Devlin tried to settle his nerves, but he had a hard time tamping down what Jenni said was a "million years of evolution" reminding him that he was human and most everyone in the park was *not*. He'd been at Amazing Adventures for a month, working in the finance department by day and sexing up his lioness soulmate at night. But right now, he was giving a presentation to the council—made up of the alphas and other important members of the shifter groups—about the finances for the park as well as an update on the apartment complex.

He was nervous because he wanted to do well for his bosses. He'd have been nervous whether they were shifters or not. Maybe.

Joss cleared his throat. The alpha wolf was a serious man and Devlin had only seen him smile twice in the last month. Jenni had explained that Joss had killed his son, after he put the entire park at risk by attacking Zane's soulmate, Adriana. Devlin couldn't imagine doing something like that to his own child, but shifters were more practical than humans, and they saw the world in different tones than he did.

"You have a report for us, Devlin?" Joss asked.

"Yes," he said, standing and carrying his laptop to the head of the conference table. The council met monthly, but could also convene to discuss important issues related to the park and their people.

Devlin plugged his laptop into the projection system while Jupiter lowered a screen on the wall for his presentation. Shaking off his nerves, he started the presentation, flipping through the slides that he'd made to explain the park's financial situation. After answering questions, he turned his attention to the apartment complex.

Clicking the next slide, he said, "The bank approved the construction loan, so we just need to choose a builder from the six bids that we accepted. We're looking at around twelve months until completion, depending on weather, supplies, and workers. The two-story building will have four apartments on each floor with exterior entrances. Each apartment will have two bedrooms and one bathroom."

Devlin detailed the different timelines and costs for each builder that had submitted a bid for the job, and the alphas voted on Vane Brothers Construction. He'd thought they were the best fit for the job, too.

"Set up a meeting for the company," Atticus said. "We'd like to meet them in person."

"And I have a number of wolves who would be available to help with construction as well," Joss said.

"I'll set something up for them next week," Devlin said.

"I think that's everything," Caesar said.

As the group dispersed, Devlin said, "Can I speak to you for a minute, Caesar?"

"Sure," he said.

Devlin unplugged his laptop and shut the lid, waiting until they were alone before he spoke.

"I'd like to ask Jenni to marry me, and since she thinks of you as a father, I wanted to get your permission."

Caesar said nothing for a long moment, and then smiled. "Of course, I approve. I wouldn't think of standing in the way of the traditions of your people, since you accepted ours so easily."

Devlin knew that shifters didn't necessarily consider marriage by human standards to be more than a piece of government-issued paper, but it was important to him that Jenni be his wife and take his last name.

"I'd like to propose after dinner on Sunday night," he said.

"That's a great idea. The pride would love to be part of it, since it's not normal for us."

"Depending on how many mates end up being human, though, I suspect that there will be a lot more proposals in the pipeline."

"True. Your sister and cousin aren't engaged yet."

"I'm sure they will be soon. Win and Justus would do anything for their mates."

"That's the way it's supposed to be."

Devlin walked out of the meeting room with Caesar, and headed topside, where he borrowed an SUV from the park and went to find a jewelry store. He'd already gathered one of Jenni's rings from her jewelry box to use for sizing. It hadn't taken him long to find the perfect ring for her—two diamonds centered on a platinum ring, with rows of tiny diamonds on either side. It was the perfect size, too.

After leaving the jewelry store, he picked up a bottle of sparkling wine for the celebration and returned to the park and back to work. He hadn't thought it was possible to like a job more than he had his previous job as assistant controller. Being the finance manager for the park was more challenging and rewarding than he ever thought possible. He was helping to ensure that the park stayed profitable so their people had a place to live. Working for the park meant he was helping to keep a roof over his sweetheart's head and to provide stability and a wonderful future for their children.

∼

Jenni thought Devlin was acting strange Sunday evening when he came to get her after the shop was closed for the day. He was smiling, but he was trying to hide just how much. He was definitely up to something, but she couldn't fathom what it might be.

"We could go out to dinner instead of eating with the pride," she suggested.

"No!" He cleared his throat and then said with less enthusiasm, "I mean that we should eat with the pride because it's one of Caesar's unspoken rules."

She hummed. "Okay. Just a suggestion."

"Tomorrow though, since it's technically the start of our weekend, I'd love to take you out."

"I'd like to try the new Italian place. I could go for some cannolis."

After arriving at their house, she showered and changed, and they walked to Caesar's house. When he opened the front door, the scent of fried chicken hit her nose and she purred at the thought of eating one of her favorite things.

Her stomach growled loudly. "Hungry?" Devlin teased.

"You know it. Plus, I love fried chicken."

"Me, too."

They joined the pride at the table and ate, conversation flowing smoothly between them all. She marveled at how easily Devlin fit into her world. He joked with the pride and they treated him as if he'd been with them for years instead of just a month. They'd even started working out together a few times a week, and she'd loved watching Devlin push himself on the weights that made his muscles bulge and filled her mind with all sorts of wicked thoughts.

She'd thought she might never find a mate, but she had, and he was perfect. Well, he *did* leave his wet towels on the bathroom floor and more often than not forgot to put his dishes in the dishwasher, but those were all things she didn't really mind because she was crazy about him. It hadn't taken long for her sexy, tattooed soulmate to burrow into her heart, but there he was. She loved him. And she couldn't wait to tell him.

The table was cleared and she pushed her chair out so they could head home, but Devlin stopped her. "Hold on, sweetheart," he said.

"What?" she asked.

He pushed his chair back and dropped to one knee. Her breath caught in her throat and every instinct within her focused on his hand and the diamond ring glittering in the overhead light.

"Jenni, I feel like we've been together for years and not just weeks. I never imagined I'd be settling down with such a beautiful woman, or that she'd be able to shift into a lioness whenever she fancied, but I can't imagine my life without you in it. I wouldn't want to go to bed without your sweet scent enveloping me, or wake up without you next to me, and I never, ever want to go back to a place where I was just existing and working, and not really living, the way that I am now that we're together. I love you with all my heart. Will you marry me?"

She stared at the ring, her vision blurring as tears filled her eyes.

"I love you, too," she whispered, her voice filled with emotion. "And yes, I will."

The pride cheered, clapping and roaring their happiness, as Devlin pushed the ring onto her finger and stood, drawing her to her feet and kissing her.

Celeste and Jupiter opened the bottle of sparkling wine that Devlin had brought, and glasses were passed around. She and Devlin sat down and she brushed at her wet cheeks. She couldn't stop smiling.

Caesar stood and lifted his glass. "Years ago, we didn't think about humans becoming our soulmates, because our people found mates within our own kind. But it's easy to see with the love between the two of you, and the other mates at the zoo, that this is a whole new chapter for our people. Welcome to the family and the pride, Devlin."

Their glasses clinked and she sipped at the sweet and bubbly drink. Resting her head on his shoulder, she said, "I love my ring."

"One diamond for you and one for me."

"And the other little diamonds?"

"How many kids we'll have."

She looked at the ring more closely. "That's a *lot* of kids."

He laughed and kissed her. "However many kids we have, our family will be amazing."

"Because we're both so awesome."

"And modest," Caesar said.

She and Devlin laughed and the pride joined in. As the conversation turned to their engagement, excitement brewed within her. Even though they were soulmates, she still wanted to be his wife, and his proposal was a dream come true. And maybe soon they'd get started on their family. Little boys with his blue eyes and infectious smile, and little girls with her blonde hair and fierce lioness nature. She hoped their kids could shift, but even if they couldn't it wouldn't matter. She'd learned something about having a soulmate—the outside package didn't matter as much as the heart, and in her mind, Devlin was as fierce and protective as any shifter she'd ever met.

He was a lion in his heart, and she loved him from head to toe.

AVAILABLE NOW IN THE WERE ZOO
SERIES
KELLEY (WERE ZOO BOOK SIX)

www.rebutlerauthor.com

CONTACT THE AUTHOR

Website: http://www.rebutlerauthor.com
Email: rebutlerauthor@gmail.com
Facebook: www.facebook.com/R.E.ButlerAuthorPage

ALSO FROM R. E. BUTLER

<u>Arctic Shifters</u>
Blitzen's Fated Mate
Dasher's Fated Mate
Prancer's Fated Mate
Vixen's Fated Mate
Cupid's Fated Mate
Dancer's Fated Mate
Donner's Fated Mate
Comet's Fated Mate

Ashland Pride
Seducing Samantha
Loving Lachlyn
Marking Melody
Redeeming Rue
Saving Scarlett
Chasing Cristabel
Jilly's Wyked Fate
Embracing Ehrin
Holding Honor

ALSO FROM R. E. BUTLER

Tempting Treasure
Having Hope

Hyena Heat
Every Night Forever
Every Dawn Forever
Every Sunset Forever
Every Blissful Moment
Every Heavenly Moment
Every Miraculous Moment
Every Angelic Moment

The Necklace Chronicles
The Tribe's Bride
The Gigolo's Bride
The Tiger's Bride
The Alpha Wolf's Mate
The Jaguar's Bride
The Author's True Mate

Norlanian Brides
Paoli's Bride
Warrick's Bride
Dex's Bride
Norlanian Brides Volume One
Villi's Bride
Dero's Bride

Saber Chronicles
Saber Chronicles Volume One (Books One - Four)

Sable Cove
Must Love Familiars

ALSO FROM R. E. BUTLER

Tails
Memory
Mercy
Emberly
AnnaRose

Uncontrollable Shift
The Alpha's Christmas Mate
The Dragon's Treasured Mate
The Bear's Reluctant Mate
The Leopard Twins' Christmas Mate

Vampire Beloved
Want
Need
Ache

Were Zoo
Zane
Jupiter
Win
Justus
Devlin
Kelley
Auden
Tayme
Joss
Neo

Wiccan-Were-Bear
A Curve of Claw
A Flash of Fang
A Price for a Princess
A Bond of Brothers

ALSO FROM R. E. BUTLER

A Bead of Blood
A Twitch of Tail
A Promise on White Wings
A Slash of Savagery
Awaken a Wolf
Daeton's Journey
A Dragon for December
A Muse for Mishka
The Wiccan-Were-Bear Series Volume One
The Wiccan-Were-Bear Series Volume Two
The Wiccan-Were-Bear Series Volume Three
A Wish for Their Woman

Wilde Creek
Volume One (Books 1 and 2)
Volume Two (Books 3 and 4)
Volume Three (Books 5 and 6)
The Hunter's Heart (Book Seven)
The Beta's Heart (Book Eight)

The Wolf's Mate
The Wolf's Mate Book 1: Jason & Cadence
The Wolf's Mate Book 2: Linus & The Angel
The Wolf's Mate Book 3: Callie & The Cats
The Wolf's Mate Book 4: Michael & Shyne
The Wolf's Mate Book 5: Bo & Reika
The Wolf's Mate Book 6: Logan & Jenna
The Wolf's Mate Book 7: Lindy & The Wulfen

Available now in the Were Zoo Series: Kelley (Were Zoo Six)

ALSO FROM R. E. BUTLER

Kelley London has been taking care of the non-shifting animals at the Amazing Adventures Safari Park since he was a kid. As an elephant shifter, he has a unique take on what it means to be an animal in the zoo, gawked at by humans, and he does his best to make sure that the animals are happy and well taken care of. He's not sure that the VIP tours are going to bring his soulmate to him, but he's hopeful that someday he'll find the one female meant to be his.

Rhapsody Caine is the last surviving member of her panther shifter pride. Before her aunt passed away, she told Rhapsody about a shifter zoo in New Jersey, and urged her to find other shifters to live with. She's never been around other types of shifters, and she's wary of just waltzing in the front gates and announcing herself to the zoo's inhabitants, so she signs up for a VIP tour of the safari. What she doesn't expect is to be staring at her soulmate through a chain link fence, or for him to be an elephant.

Rhapsody breaks all the rules and climbs the fence during the tour to be with Kelley, but the big male doesn't care that she's impetuous. The only thing he cares about is that she's the new center of his universe, and because she's all alone in the world, he wants to become her family. When a panther male shows up at the zoo, claiming to be Rhapsody's arranged mate, Kelley is willing to fight for his claim to the beautiful female.

Printed in Great Britain
by Amazon